TWICE *Betrayed*

CARLA TUCKER MINKS

ISBN 978-1-956010-54-1 (paperback)
ISBN 978-1-956010-55-8 (digital)

Rushmore Press LLC
1 800 460 9188
www.rushmorepress.com

Printed in the United States of America

Acknowledgements

I worked on the original manuscript far longer than I ever anticipated. Signing with Rushmore Press to republish *Twice Betrayed* granted me the opportunity to edit and update the story and provide a better foundation for the long-awaited sequel. The delays came amidst deaths, surgeries, cancer, illness, several moves, and unemployment— not all my experiences, but my voyage, nonetheless.

Throughout both of my writing journeys on this book, my cheerleaders included Sue, I pray you're resting peacefully, Marylou, always supporting me, and Jeannine, a writer drafting her first novel. My deepest of gratitude to these amazing women for standing with me all this time. The sequel is well underway, so the wait will not take another nine years. Oh, I surely hope not!

In the meantime, I wrote and published a series of children's books focused on learning and growth opportunities entitled *The Adventures of Petey the Chiweenie*. Please check them out online and remember to leave reviews so my books will be found more easily.

Thank you all and enjoy the story about Taylor Calloway in *Twice Betrayed*.

"Chelsea PD: Public asked to help locate missing man."

The headline was like a punch to the gut—Calvin was truly gone. His wife and my best friend, Annette, was broken. Where love and enthusiasm once reigned, she was consumed by despair. She had lost all sense of time, experienced uncontrollable bouts of sobbing, weak knees, and loss of strength to even support herself when standing. Annette regularly whispered "Oh God" toward the heavens as if expecting an answer.

Annette spoke of nothing else but Calvin for the first year. She stopped eating and drove the streets of Chelsea, stopped at every bar, and walked the shoreline in search of her husband. By the second year, she ceased talking at all and she carried a vacant look with slack facial expressions. Annette avoided people and social situations. She simply disappeared.

As her closest friend, I was lost as to how I could comfort her when the only thing she desired was her husband's return home alive and well. I cooked meals for her, walked the beaches in silence, sat on her patio late into the night; sometimes until dawn when her routine repeated.

As she mourned the loss of her husband, I grieved the loss of my friend, a woman I'd known nearly all my life. On the fifth anniversary of Calvin's disappearance, she replaced her sweats with jeans and shirts, cut and colored her hair, and began eating on her own once more. It seemed she was clawing her way out of the gloom in search of sunlight instead of Calvin's lost body.

Out of the blue one day, Annette leased a space in downtown Chelsea for a clothing shop. She had not mentioned this idea before the ink was dry on the contract, but my friend was a stylish woman with an eye for trends and matching body shapes with clothing that emphasized the most flattering features. She needed income by now, so she decided on a venture into fashion in our small beach community.

By the opening day of Four Season's Boutique, Calvin James was not mentioned. Annette no longer spoke his name and focused her energy on her future as a single woman. She didn't identify as a widow or abandoned person; she just knew her future was on her own, so why not on her own terms? As her best friend, I dedicated my free time to helping her get the store open and marketed. Annette was coming alive again. As a therapist, I was thrilled by her growth and determination to find happiness once more, even if it was without her husband.

But this isn't my story, nor is it the end or the beginning. I am merely a therapist in the lovely town of Chelsea, a small beach community on the west coast. No, my story, my existence, is wrapped up in the many lives that seek out my services to find answers and understanding about challenging person's situations.

Over the course of my adult years, I have spoken with thousands of people from all lifestyles and corners of the globe about all of life's offerings: birthdays, families, boyfriends, girlfriends, husbands, wives, children, pets, death, periods, traumas, food, work, education, and sex. There have been lots of talk about sex. I find it most intriguing to hear about these women's lives and enjoy their endless ruminations. Sometimes though, I have difficulty relating to their views and experiences. I suppose one would call me a conventionalist, but I am not surprised by their bizarre life lessons. I have never fantasized about being a celebrity or being wealthy or saving all of humanity by developing a super-drug. I wanted to be a college graduate who married a nice guy and moved to suburbia where we raised our two children. Sound familiar? Perhaps blasé?

Reviewing my life now, I would say that my tailored life has offered nearly all that I hoped it would. I have listened intently and hypnotically as men and women, some close friends, share with me their aspirations of a life full of experience, achievement, and intrigue. I often find myself absorbed into their worlds as they speak with the giddiness of deceit, secrets, and abundant sweltering passion— passions no longer shared with their spouses, but with other men or women they have on the side.

I am not one for judging others for their beliefs or even their actions; yet I am curious about how they developed them. I ask piercing questions like when did you first think about that? Where were you when you first tried that? Who encouraged you? How did you know to do it that way? My existence, at times, seems so narrow and mainstream that I do not believe I've earned the right to instill ordinances on others.

Though I was raised in a conservatively middle-class family with a reasonable understanding of life and its contrasts, I do not react with shock or disgust to stories of sexual encounters behind the local bowling alley or in the bathroom of a friend's home during a holiday party. I do not recall even catching my breath when hearing about Lacy narrowly escaping exposure while orally satisfying the PTA president under the bleachers one Friday night. Intrigue and fascination motivate me to learn more about the people living in the homes of my town. I sit in the local coffee shop and imagine what the man next to me is dealing with that day. Where did he come from? Where was he going next? Whom did he know that I also knew? Did he have sex this morning? Was it with his wife? Is she now with another man? At times, I question my lack of desire for a deeper propensity for mystery and erotica in my own relationship.

It's not surprising then that I chose the field of psychology to study. I had known since my freshman year of high school that human behavior was my interest. My decision never wavered, and I worked to that goal with persistence. I also knew that I would never leave Chelsea, so my options would be somewhat limited to private practice, a neighboring psychiatric hospital, or teaching. Since my level of curiosity about people ran remarkably high, private practice was my ambition. There had been a period of time before graduating from the university when I entertained teaming with a classmate, but she eventually set her sights down South, so I resurrected Plan A.

Because of the nature of the work, it's not uncommon for therapists to seek out mentors to stay grounded and neutral. The mentor I chose was Brett Maxey, an alum and psychiatrist who teaches specialized psych courses at the university, maintains a small practice, and consults at the psychiatric hospital and rehab center. Just how he manages to balance these responsibilities and fit in a round of golf each week inspires me. In addition to these obligations, he connects with me each Wednesday, sometimes by phone if I have little to discuss.

The rest of my week is consumed with the traditional fifty-minute therapy sessions in my small corner office above the market and dress shop. My day typically begins at nine o'clock with an extended lunch from noon to one-thirty, followed by more sessions. Some of my clients are regulars with standing weekly appointments, while many more have bi-weekly or monthly appointments. A handful of my clients struggle with mental disorders that require medication to stabilize their behaviors or chemical imbalances, and several others battle addictions, such as alcohol, drug, and/or sexual compulsions. The remainder of my clientele is seeking help with relationships, managing stress or anger, and a small number just want someone to talk to about their lives in and around Chelsea.

Outside my office door hangs a simply engraved sign that reads: Taylor Calloway, Psychotherapist. Upon opening the outer door, visitors enter a small but inviting waiting room. The décor is straight out of the Pottery Barn catalog with four armchairs upholstered in a sagebrush twill fabric and two small side tables stained in a rich espresso finish. Each table is adorned with a mission-style iron lamp and a couple of current magazines suitable for both genders: *Sports Illustrated, O, Coastal Living,* and *Travel and Leisure.* The walls are painted a soft gray blue to keep my clients feeling calm. The floor throughout this space is carpeted and I have laid a natural jute rug in this area for a touch of texture. The artwork consists of black and white scenes from the surrounding area, courtesy of Annette. The next door is my office and where I see clients. Two more armchairs, a couch in a complementary harbor blue stripe, a contemporary coffee table, also in espresso finish, and another rug are arranged in the center of the room. A small desk is in the far-right corner near a set of windows for good lighting and a view of the ocean.

I boot up the computer atop my desk and I check my calendar for the day's schedule.

CHELSEA

The alarm rings at five-forty-five in the morning. My husband, Jake, is sound asleep, softly snoring to my right, and Cali, our sweet mongrel dog, is curled up at the end of the bed with her head resting on my feet. Without opening my eyes, I reach out toward the clock radio and press the snooze button thinking that ten more minutes will magically rejuvenate my lagging energy for the day ahead. Upon hearing the second alarm, Cali is up and ready to get to her backyard for a few laps around the perimeter in search of foreign invaders before breakfast is served.

Like a drone, I throw the blankets off and slowly roll out of the large bed. Jake does not stir. My slippers shuffle across the hardwood floor while Cali runs circles around me. I open the back door and like a dart, she bolts to the center of the grass. The aroma of hot strong coffee lures me to the kitchen. I fill the cup that was placed next to the coffee maker the night before and take a cautious sip. Heading back to the master bathroom, I look forward to the warm shower that will awaken me for my daily routine. Another morning has begun.

The town of Chelsea is neither large nor small with a population of less than 35,000 people. Its location offers a nice compromise of the ocean to the west and foothills for hiking to the east. The downtown streets are lined with well-manicured Natchez Crape Myrtle trees. Bright, beautiful flower mixtures fill containers along the sides. This welcoming sight is complimented by a slow and easy pace, so unlike many other beach cities along the Pacific coast. Somehow, in its zeal to acquire and mass-produce chains of stores and hotels, corporate America has fortunately overlooked Chelsea. Downtown activity hums with the energy of small retailers, cozy restaurants, and tourists all year long. Most of the visitors to Chelsea are lodged in bed and breakfasts, which helps to maintain a charming, small-town feel the residents prefer.

Like most mornings, my first stop is The Perk on Main and Fourth where I meet Linda for coffee before going to our respective offices. Linda and I have been friends for more than fifteen years and yet, conversations never get too personal or too intimate. Talk is general chit-chat and typically includes family events, weekend plans, work gossip, and the like. We share recipes, new make-up finds, catalog buys, and birthday party planning. Our husbands even get together and golf a couple of times a month at the local course. They are part of our extended family.

During this morning's conversation, Linda discusses a grant that she is pursuing to support a local university program she manages in the English department. The submission deadline is fast approaching and, as usual, she has postponed the work. She'll need to devote her nights and the next few weekends to pull her proposal together. She laughs and confesses, "I do this with every grant." I offer my standard assistance that she acknowledges but rebuffs. It's just a fact that Linda performs best under pressure, which is very good for her because she puts things off regularly more often than I buy handbags. As a master procrastinator, she's a twenty-first-century Scarlet O'Hara.

At eight-thirty, we hug and say goodbye outside the coffee house. Linda is heading to her office at the university, while I walk just a few blocks to a stone and cedar building, which houses a small market, dress shop, and a couple of office suites on the second level. Ten years ago, I was lucky to stumble upon this corner space where I set up a private practice. I am one of less than a dozen therapists in Chelsea and business is comfortably busy. My practice consists mostly of local women, some men, and just a few restless teens.

Along my walk south on Fourth Street, I pass friendly business owners readying for another day. Sidewalks are being swept, tables and chairs wiped down, windows being cleaned, and merchandise being neatly displayed to lure in customers. As I stroll down the walk, I too am preparing myself for a new day that may bring its own surprising conversations in my small office just ahead on Seaside Road.

Before ascending the stairs to the second level of the Hampton Building where my office is located, I enter the Four Seasons Boutique owned by my good friend, Annette. We've been close since the age of three or four and I adore her. She was the person who gave me the lead on the office space above her store a decade ago and so we share a few minutes each morning before the crowds of tourists and residents gathers on the streets of downtown Chelsea.

"Good morning!" I call out as I enter the store and Annette appears from behind a rack of new summer dresses that arrived the day before.

"You have got to look at this new line I'm carrying," she says with excitement. Annette is always dressed in free-flowing, comfortable, and artfully colorful attire. She has an instinct for piecing together outfits that best suit any personality or occasion and I remain her biggest style challenge. Each day, I dress in slacks and a button-down oxford or a long skirt and tunic in neutral or soft shades. I am conservative and opt for easy care in my everyday outfits.

"There is a rose-colored, sleeveless dress with a green belt here in your size," Annette continues without looking up. As she pulls the item from the rack, she gives it a little shake as though to mesmerize me into taking the bait. I smile, "You know, I just may come back down around lunch and try it on." Annette knows better and gently shakes her head as she hangs it back in its place.

I weave through the racks of clothes to Annette and hand her a coffee cup from The Perk. It is my morning gesture that she welcomes with genuine anticipation. "Ah, thank you."

Annette is a loving, outgoing, and artistic woman who genuinely enjoys interacting with others, especially women. Her height and weight are average, but she has gentle, chocolate brown eyes that draw people to her. Like most, Annette's life has had its share of hardship. For example, she was married years ago to a man who emotionally abused and then abandoned her. Her husband, Calvin, left one day and never returned or called. After three years of searching and worrying, she just stopped mentioning his name and went on with her life. She is a woman of unbridled inner strength that is anchored by a strong faith in God, her family, and her close friends. Annette is a gift in my life that I am thankful for every day.

"My photography is being featured in the art department's annual show at the university next month and I want you to come with me. Promise me you will." My BFF stares me down until I respond.

"Of course, I'll be your date! Text the details to me so I can get it on my calendar." At ten minutes to nine, I give her a hug and wish her a great day then leave the store. Before ascending the stairs to the second level, a chill runs up my spine and the hair on the back of my neck stand on edge stopping me from moving any further. Is someone watching me? My eyes review the area for something or someone out of place but there is nothing. I shake off the unnerving awareness then continue up the concrete stairs to my awaiting office.

Cathie

My first appointment most Monday mornings is with Cathie, an attractive middle-aged woman whom I first met three years prior. She was in the midst of her fourth divorce and needed someone who would listen to her vent because, as she said, "I have worn out the compassion of my so-called friends." Cathie married wealthy men and accumulated quite a fortune through real estate sales and each divorce. She has two high-school-aged children from unions one and two and surrenders to their every demand. Cathie has yet to admit that she lives in a constant state of fear: she is afraid of growing old, of losing her children, and is most terrified of being alone.

At precisely nine o'clock, Cathie takes a seat in her usual spot on the couch nearest my chair. Her hair and makeup are flawless, and she is impeccably dressed in a new outfit from Chico's.

"You look beautiful today, Cathie," I say. "How are things going with you?"

Cathie is quiet for a few minutes before a smile grows on her lips. "I met someone this weekend." She sits back into the cushions of the couch, wraps her arms around herself, and gives a gentle hug. "I met him at the Club Saturday night." The club is the local yacht club where the wealthy gather to be among their equals—rich and beautiful.

Still smiling, she says, "He sent two dozen roses this morning and, I know we talked about taking relationships one step at a time, but he could be the one."

Oh goodness, I think, there it is—number five?

I possess a profound interest in knowing the meaning of names and my reference website defines "Cathy" as pure and I would agree with this for the woman who sits before me. To a fault, Cathie is not a bitter or vengeful person and, for the most part, she is quite optimistic. She lives to love others and desperately wants to be loved back. She has a very romantic image of love and marriage; a 1950s version of coupleship that places the man as the leader of the household. Cathie wants to take care of a man and provide a nice home, and all she wants in return is to be cherished by him. And she wants her man to be faithful, successful, and a couple of years younger than herself.

"His name is Nathan, and he is looking for a property here in Chelsea." Cathie begins turning the diamond ring on her right middle finger, a habit she has when she is feeling particularly vulnerable. "He is a friend of Dana Richards, the attorney. Do you know him?" I do not and silently indicate so.

"Who did you go to the club with Saturday night?" I ask. Cathie has agreed to take a girlfriend when she goes to parties. The "buddy system" is intended to help keep her feet on the ground and she is not to leave a party with any man no matter how taken she is with him. She is learning to take relationships slowly and to allow the man the lead role in the courtship.

"I went with Pamela. She and I had a wonderful time. She thought Nathan was perfect, too." Cathie smiles again, this time with a flush of rose across her cheeks. "I gave him my phone number and we're going to dinner at The Cliffs this Friday night." I could see the wheels turning. "Maybe he will let me show him around our beautiful town and help him get settled in."

Time to reel her in, I think. "Let's talk about ground rules for Friday night. What have we agreed to in the past?" I ask.

"I know. I know. I'm projecting too far into the future. We haven't even had our first date!" Cathie exclaims, sounding as though this is new information just dawning on her. "I'm going to let Nathan take the lead and I'm just going to enjoy myself. And when he takes me back home, I'm going to thank him for a wonderful time then send him on his way. I promise not to ask him to stay the night." Cathie doesn't sound too convincing, but that isn't the point.

"We want to work on courting and intimacy before sex," I add. "As you build a relationship and it feels right, then allow things to progress to the next step. On your terms when you feel ready." I give her a reassuring smile.

"On my terms. When I feel emotionally ready," Cathie repeats with a nod. "You know, I just don't like being alone," she admits.

There it is, the most honest statement Cathie could make. "I understand, but we've got to be strong individuals, comfortable with who we are before we submerge ourselves into intimate relationships with others. It's the true love and respect that we have for ourselves that allow us to remain whole and intact as part of a couple. You don't want to disappear into another man's shadow."

"No, I do not," Cathie says with conviction. "I want to be strong and comfortable being me. I want to be loved for who I am."

I can see tears welling in her soft blue eyes as she begins to fan her face. I reach for a tissue and hand it to her to dab the moisture from her cheeks. She is an overly sensitive and vulnerable woman struggling with independence.

"I'll have lots to talk about with you next week." She stands, tidies herself, and applies another layer of lipstick before opening the office door to leave. "Wish me luck, Taylor."

"You don't need me to wish you luck. Have a wonderful week, Cathie. I'll see you again next Monday."

With that, Cathie is out the door and on her way.

I jot a few notes in Cathie's file before hearing the outer door open. Time for my ten o'clock, I think as I stand to greet my new client.

GABRIEL

After lunch, I hear the door. A man stands uncertainly. "Hi, Gabriel," I say, smiling and shaking his hand. "Come in and make yourself comfortable. Sit anywhere you like."

Gabriel looks somewhat familiar. Maybe I'd seen him around town or at a party sometime. He is handsome and quite tall with curly sand-colored hair and soft hazel eyes. He is casually dressed in khaki shorts and a t-shirt with a surf shop logo imprint. Gabriel has raised his sunglasses to just above the hairline on his forehead and he nervously rolls his keys from one hand to the other until he takes a seat.

Gabriel: God is my strength. I wonder if he is praying now? Then I close the door and join my new client in the chair across from him.

"Gabriel, I'm Taylor and I've been in private practice here in Chelsea for the past ten years." I watch him as he becomes aware of the keys in his hands, and then places them on the coffee table between us. "What brings you to see me?" I ask.

Gabriel looks at me then away, scanning the room. He takes a breath then looks at me again. "I thought I was having a heart attack a couple of weeks ago, but it turned out to be anxiety. The shrink on-call suggested I see a therapist and he gave me your name and number." He had begun running his hands down his thighs. Two, three, four times he lifts his hands, places them at the tops of his legs, and then pushes them slowly toward his knees. Then he stops, leaving the palms resting on his shorts.

"I haven't been sleeping very well for a long time," he confesses. "Dr. Maxey said you could help me relax."

Ah, a Brett Maxey referral. "I work very closely with Dr. Maxey; we go way back to college." Gabriel acknowledges my words with a slow nod.

"Why don't you tell me a little bit about yourself? Do you live in Chelsea? What do you do? Just a little background to help me get to know you." My tone is calm and filled with sincere interest.

"Okay. Um, well, I grew up down South and moved here about seven years ago. I own a surfboard business with a couple of buddies. Well, just one guy now. We do alright, I guess. I mean, business is steady." He adjusts his position in the chair then continues. "I've never done this before, never been to a therapist." He looks down at the table shyly. It wasn't uncommon, especially for men, to feel ashamed to seek help.

"It's very normal to feel uncomfortable at first, Gabriel. Hopefully, over time, you will trust me, and the nervousness will subside." I give him a gentle smile and continue, "You said that you've had trouble sleeping for 'a long time.' How long has it been?" I ask, hoping that a less personal question will allow him to relax.

Gabriel takes a deep breath and eases back into the chair. "Years. It's been years since I was able to fall asleep and stay unconscious till morning." He again adjusts himself in the chair and runs a hand through his hair.

"So, you have trouble falling asleep and staying asleep?" I pause to give Gabriel the opportunity to respond. After he nods, I continue. "Tell me about your typical day."

Gabriel looks up at the ceiling and shrugs. "A typical day? I get up around six and go surfing for an hour or two then I shower and go to the shop. Around four-thirty or five, I either hit the beach again or go with Wes for a couple of beers before picking up dinner and heading home." He shrugs again.

"Okay, that's good," I say reassuringly. "Do you drink on a daily basis?"

"I don't know, maybe two beers, nothing hard. I'm not an alcoholic." Gabriel sounds defensive and catches himself, "Anything we talk about is confidential. Right?"

"That's right. I want you to be open and honest with me. Anything you share stays between us. Think of this office as Vegas." I continue, "Do you use any drugs?"

Gabriel leans forward resting his elbows on his knees and starts tapping one foot quietly on the floor. "I smoke a little weed on the weekends. You know, partying with friends."

"You said that you surfed; is there any other physical activity you do regularly?" I ask.

Gabriel sits back in the chair and relaxes. "I do lots of stuff with my buddies on the weekends," he said. "We go biking in the hills, shoot hoops, play a little golf, and sail."

I can see by looking at him that he is in good physical condition with toned muscles and a slim physique.

"I like to be outdoors, and I like to stay busy."

"That all sounds great to me," I add. "What about relationships? You've mentioned 'buddies' a couple of times and Wes. Are you dating or married?"

"I see a couple of ladies but nothing too serious. I guess I'm just not ready to settle down."

"It could also be that you haven't met the right person yet. Good relationships can't be manufactured at will. Just take your time and stay tuned into your feelings. I think we have other areas to focus on for now, like getting to the source of your insomnia." Another smile and nod.

"You mentioned that you co-own a surf shop in town. That alone can cause sleepless nights. You know, worrying about income, orders, keeping customers happy. How's your relationship with your partner? Is there stress there that may contribute feeling anxious?" I ask.

"Nah, we're good. I don't know Wes as well as my buddy who started the shop, but we're getting along great. Wes stays on the customer service side of things, and I build the boards. He has a good eye for design and improving the performance of the surfboards and it's been fun working with new materials. We're good." Gabriel sounds more relaxed sharing information about the shop.

"That's not always the case, so it's great to hear that you're compatible. So, we'll start our work on helping you get more rest. My suggestion is that you cut out drinking alcohol too late in the evening and switch to water or decaffeinated teas. Okay?"

Gabriel nods with agreement.

"And try meditating before you crawl into bed."

Gabriel sits back with his shoulders against the chair.

"Don't panic. This just means sitting quietly for fifteen to thirty minutes to clear your mind of lingering thoughts that may disrupt your sleep. How does that sound?" I ask.

"I'd like that," Gabriel acknowledges. "So, how often do I need to come here? I mean, how many times a week or month?"

"Let's try once a week for now. Will this same day and time work for you?" I ask.

"Sure. Whatever we need to do." I can hear a dash of relief in his voice as he stands to leave. He looks at me and adds, "Thanks. This wasn't as bad as I thought it was going to be."

"I'm awfully glad to hear that, Gabriel. We'll do what we can to get you in a better place. In the meantime, I'd like you to start keeping a journal. Have you ever kept a journal?" I ask.

Gabriel furls his brow and purses his lips then shakes his head.

"This will help you deal more constructively with feelings of anxiety and panic and help identify the triggers. Next week, we'll explore breathing and relaxation techniques that will assist you in dealing with these uncomfortable feelings. How does that sound so far?"

My client tilts his head, "So far?"

"I'd also like you to keep track of your daily activities and your sleep pattern. Just keep a notepad by your bed and jot down the times you go to bed and the times that you wake up. Oh, and write down the dreams and the thoughts you have as soon as you wake up. Does this sound like something you would be willing to do?"

Gabriel nods, and with that, I walk him to the door. "See you next week."

ABIGAIL

I am sitting at my small antique desk near the windows of my office wrapping up notes from Gabriel's first visit when the phone rings. A quick glance at the caller I.D. and I recognize the number to be Brett's cell phone.

"Good morning, Brett, you have great timing," I say hoping to leave a bit of intrigue in the air.

"Thanks for the compliment so early in the day. What's up with you?" Brett's voice is friendly and deep, and he speaks with a hypnotic melodic cadence.

"I've just seen a man you referred to me a couple of weeks ago. You may remember his name, Gabriel Hennessey. He presented in the E.R. thinking he was having a heart attack, but it turned out to be anxiety," I say and pause to give Brett the chance to recall the patient. "We've scheduled weekly visits for now."

"Oh yes, a nice man but wound a bit too tight. I'm glad to hear he followed up with you. I wasn't convinced he would." Brett says.

"Well, you called me. What's on your mind?" I ask.

"Yeah. Are we still on for our Wednesday meeting?"

"Absolutely, if you still have time for me." My curiosity is raised since Brett doesn't normally confirm our standing appointment. "Of course. But I was thinking of meeting at Christof's instead of the University. Say, twelve-thirty? I'll have Patrice make the reservation."

He has my attention. "Christof's? What's the occasion?" I query. Christof's is a quaint, extremely popular restaurant located at the end of the pier. I've only dined there with Jake for special occasions in the past.

"No occasion, just have something I want to tell you about. Something that just came to my attention. Don't worry about it. We'll chat on Wednesday. Okay?"

"Sounds great. It'll be a nice change of pace."

"Have a good one then and I'll see you in a couple of days," Brett says cheerfully.

"You too. Ciao," I say and hear the phone line disconnect. I sit with the receiver to my ear for another minute or so speculating and wondering what this is all about. Then I hear the outer door of my office suite open, and I return the phone to its cradle.

"Hi, Taylor. Sorry, I'm late, but I slept through my alarms." The familiar voice is that of my next client, Abigail. She is young and intelligent and is our mayor's only daughter.

At five feet eleven, Abigail is tall and strikingly gorgeous. She is thin, tan, and naturally blond with piercing aqua-blue eyes that capture your gaze and make it nearly impossible to look away. At eighteen, she is bored with school, the local boys, and her privileged life.

Abigail glides into the office wearing fashionably short-shorts, tank top, and bejeweled sandals. She sets her coffee mug and Lexus keys on the coffee table then plops herself onto the center cushion of the couch. She removes the large dark sunglasses and lays them on the table with her other belongings.

I have been seeing Abigail for four months now, beginning only two months after her mother, Teena, committed suicide. Abigail had been at the mall with friends and was running late. She had planned to stop at the house briefly to freshen up before heading out again to a party where she was to meet Justin—the hunk of the week. Abigail had made a couple of calls from the mall to home and to her mom's cell phone to remind her that she needed her favorite outfit washed and ready for her, but Teena never answered either phone and Abigail had become aggravated, and the last message was short and demanding. When she arrived home to find her mother's lifeless body, Abigail fell apart. The guilt over the anger she had expressed manifested into a depression that led to partying and drinking too hard. She lost all interest in school and began acting out sexually.

Abigail had been an honor student at Chelsea High and was on track to graduate a year early. She was a cheerleader and the lead female in every school play. She had an aptitude for mathematics and modeled on the side. Abigail's mother had acted more like her friend than her maternal figure and didn't administer any discipline, but Abigail was a good daughter who rarely stepped out of bounds. Losing her mother, her best friend, was devastating and Abigail simply wanted to give up. She dropped out of all her extra-curricular activities, pulled away from many of her girlfriends, and stopped planning for college at Stanford in the fall.

It had been Abigail's father, Johnston, who made the arrangements for her therapy. "I don't care what it takes. Just get her through this. I couldn't survive losing my little girl, too," he had pleaded with tears in his eyes.

"Abigail, it's really good to see you. How have you been the past couple of weeks?" I ask as I settle into my chair and give her a warm sincere smile.

"I've been alright. Graduation is Friday. Finally. Seniors finished with classes last week, so we don't need to show up at all this week." Abigail reclines on the couch, making herself very comfortable as always. "I just don't get what all the fuss is about."

"The fuss is about you. It's about the hard work you've accomplished and the future that is ahead of you." I can see the pain in her eyes. "Your mom is always with you, Abigail. You know how proud she was of you, and you know she wanted you to go to college and be spectacular there, too."

Abigail releases a heavy sigh. "I don't know that I can go to graduation without her there. She would have been so excited and would have embarrassed me when they announced my name." She picks up a small pillow and holds it close. "It just won't be a big deal now."

"It's a big deal for your dad, I assure you," I say.

Neither of us speaks for a few moments then Abigail asks what she had been asking since she found her mother. "Why did she do this to me?"

As far as I knew, Teena had not left a note explaining her suicide and this left my young client in a gaping hole to climb out of. Without an explanation, without understanding, she is struggling to move ahead.

"I don't know why, Abigail. Your mom must have been in so much pain or turmoil that she didn't see another option for herself. But it wasn't about you." I paused momentarily. "Have you talked with your dad? Asked him if he could shed any details?"

"Dad won't talk to me about Mom. He barely talks at all anymore. And I really only see him in the morning before we each head out to do our own things." She shrugs then rolls onto her side facing me.

"Well, it's not your responsibility to figure this out. Your job is to come to terms with the incident as best as you can and continue to live your life. Your mom would want you to move forward."

Abigail remains silent.

"What about your friends? During our last meeting, you agreed to call one friend each day and to go out to lunch or see a movie or something at least once a week. How is that going?"

"I'm doing well," Abigail responds then sits up. "I talk to Geri and Trisha every day and we've all gone out a couple of times. I even went with Justin to see *Sweeney Todd* at the university. It made me kind of miss the drama group at school; it was a really good performance." Her eyes twinkle for the first time since my meetings began with her.

"That is excellent! Keep it up. Remember, 'act as if and the feelings will follow.' The more fun and nurturing you are with yourself, the better you will feel and the easier it will be."

We chat about Justin and Stanford and other teenage priorities before our session ends.

"I'll see you again in two weeks, but if you need to call or come in sooner, just holler." I smile. "I'm so proud of you, Abigail."

Abigail pops up from the couch and gives me a big hug. "Thanks, Taylor. I'll see you!" She gathers her things, glides to the door, and then she is gone.

"Baby steps," I whisper to the empty room.

MARRIAGE

A quick check of voice messages before heading out for lunch. One. Jake calling to tell me he'd be getting home late . . . again. He is working late often these days, as many as three times a week. Jake was recently made head of the English Department at the university, and we knew that the promotion would require more of his time and attention.

I call Jake's office to let him know that I'd gotten his message. "Hi, babe. Sorry about tonight," Jake said, sounding distracted. "We didn't have anything planned. Did we?"

"Just the usual dinner and TV, I suppose. What's come up for you?"

"Oh, I need to catch up with one of the professors before the term ends. You remember John Knowles? He has a student appealing a grade, so we're going to review everything. You know, dot the I's and cross all the T's."

"Well, Cali and I will miss you. Hopefully, you won't be too late though. I love you."

"I'll get home as early as I can. I gotta run now. Love you." The phone line goes dead and for a moment, I sit feeling dumbfounded by the abrupt ending of the call.

Jake captured my heart during my third year in college. He stood six feet and two inches tall with broad shoulders that have a slight curve to them from his many years of swimming. Jake's walk is unrushed and lumbering and his shy smile and ocean blue eyes always make me weak in the knees. I can never stay mad at Jake, no matter the argument or disagreement, and I willingly surrender to his every kiss and yearning touch.

Though we had always talked about holding off marriage until I had completed my master's degree, we said our vows one month after I graduated with my BS in Psychology. Jake was deep into his post-graduate studies and had a teaching position lined up at the local community college. The ceremony took place before the Justice of the Peace on a Friday in June. Jake and I each had a witness present; Linda stood up for me, Rick for Jake. Two years after meeting at our wedding, Linda and Rick married in an intimate church ceremony.

At the beginning of our fourth year together, we purchased a renovated Arts and Crafts style home we still share today. We both fell in love with it the moment our eyes saw it; walking through the rooms was just a formality. The interior is accented by dark mahogany trim, hardwood floors, and warm, muted paint tones. I can't imagine living in any other home or with anyone but Jake.

We have been married twelve years and though we tried to have a child, I couldn't seem to sustain a pregnancy and miscarried four times before giving up the effort. If it was meant to be, it would happen on its own. I surrendered. That was five years ago and though the disappointment never really dissipated, I accepted that we probably would remain a childless couple. Regardless, we settled into our home and comfortably into one another.

Jake has been a thoughtful, caring partner. He remembers special occasions without hints or prompting and I never mind the predictable gifts of flowers or jewelry. And I especially don't mind taking on the role of event coordinator for organizing dinners out or excursions, but they have become fewer over the past couple of years. Jake uses work as his excuse for lack of time, but he still manages the occasional weekend spent with the guys playing in the nearby hills.

Vacations for me have become jaunts with girlfriends, usually Annette or Linda, and I prefer getting further from the local foothills. My getaways are spent across the Atlantic in Europe for an overdose of museums, churches, and castles. I love the history and architecture that foreign countries provide. These travels rejuvenate me and give me an excuse to practice my remedial foreign languages and amateur photography skills.

Life in Chelsea has been fulfilling and easy. The only drama I encounter is in my office being lived out by my clients and I prefer it that way. I don't need chaos to feel alive—a walk on the beach awakens my spirit just fine.

I lock the office door behind me and descend the steps to the sidewalk that is now bustling with people. I make a quick stop in Annette's boutique and find her behind the register finishing up a sale. When the customer has left the store, I invite her to the house for dinner.

"Jake is working late tonight. Do you want to come by for dinner? Something on the grill?"

"Working late again?" Annette asks and I nod. "Sure. Sounds tasty. I'll bring some wine and we can gossip." She smiles and winks mischievously.

"Sounds perfect. I'll see you around six-thirty." I am out on the sidewalk again heading to the market next door when the sense of being watched hits me again. Chills and hair roots jump to attention. A scan of my surroundings finds nothing unusual. I shake off the uncertainty and continue on my way.

Sweet Wheat Market is small but offers a great variety of fresh and organic foods. They make the best smoothies in town, and I am a regular during the week. Fresh fruit, soy milk, vanilla yogurt, a drizzle of honey or chocolate syrup, and ice and I have a delicious, portable lunch.

Some days, like this day, I enjoy spending thirty minutes or so planted on a bench adjacent to the beach so I can watch the people. The fresh air clears my head and tourists can be quite entertaining.

I make a mental list of the items I'll need from the market for dinner, then my mind wanders back to my phone call with Brett. *He has something to tell me that just came to his attention.* Intriguing. Perhaps he just learned of a conference coming up. Maybe, but he could have just mentioned that over the phone. My curiosity has been raised and I will need to wait another forty-eight hours to solve the mystery.

~ 26 ~

I spend the early hours of Wednesday morning reviewing and updating client files. Coffee from The Perk was to-go because Linda was unable to meet again this morning and I assume she is busy working on the grant submission since the deadline is just around the corner.

In a few hours, I will be meeting Brett at Christof's for lunch and conversation. He is a strikingly handsome man originally from Tennessee. He's tall with a thin but toned physique. Brett was blessed with thick brown hair of waves and soft curls that he leaves natural with little fuss. His eyes are green and are enhanced by the metal frames of his glasses. He mentioned once that he was considering having Lasik surgery and I tried imagining him without the distraction of glasses, then dismissed the thought when I find myself drifting towards fantasizing.

Brett left the Volunteer State to attend Stanford on an athletic scholarship and performed quite well, graduating at the top of his class. He was dedicated to his studies and obtained his Ph.D. with accolades then stepped immediately into a very prestigious job at the university before opening his own practice on the side.

When asked why he hasn't married, Brett replies, "It seems the best are taken." He typically attends functions and social events solo, and he knows most of the other guests and mingles easily but is usually among the first to leave. He dates regularly but the relationships never develop into anything meaningful and are over within months.

At twelve-fifteen, I leave my office for the short walk to Christof's at the end of the Chelsea pier. Another perfect day of sunshine, cloudless blue sky, and the temperature comfortably steady in the mid-seventies. The weather is unlike yesterday and the day before that and what one can expect for tomorrow. As I walk, I listen to the familiar sounds of beach activity: seagulls culling, children laughing, and waves rolling upon one another onto the shore. *Another perfect day,* I think as I pull the door open to the restaurant at precisely twelve-thirty.

Upon entering the restaurant lobby, my eyes fall upon Brett standing near the hostess station. He nods my way and smiles as he approaches and gives me a hug.

"Waiting long?" I ask.

"Nah. Traffic was a breeze, so I got here in no time."

On cue, the hostess motions for us to follow her to our awaiting table next to large windows. White linens, white place settings, contemporary silverware, and goblets filled with chilled water and lemon wedges contrast nicely against the ocean view through the glass. "You can't get this in Tennessee," I say kidding.

"No, ma'am. You certainly cannot," Brett responds with his best Southern drawl that he seems to have lost after so many years living on the West coast.

The hostess smiles upon hearing the charming Southern twang then shares with us the specials of the day. One-page menus are placed in our hands and as she leaves us, "Enjoy your meals."

A few moments pass as we scan the menus and chat about the choices. Then the server arrives with a basket of freshly baked sourdough bread and takes our orders. As we wait for our glasses of Chardonnay, we make small talk about our summer plans. Brett has made arrangements to travel to the east coast to visit extended family and work on a journal article. Me? I haven't scheduled anything just yet.

While we dine, we talk easily about our practices and an upcoming conference in San Francisco that I am still on the fence about attending. Brett suggests carpooling up the coast and adds, "You know that it's been several years since you attended this one. You might find the topic interesting this year and Roz Shepard is the keynote. I'll e-mail the information to you then you can tell me what you decide."

Roz Shepard is a local celebrity of sorts among mental health professionals. She established herself as a psychiatrist who gets positive results using some of the most innovative approaches to working one on one with individuals, and with groups that employ hands-on experiential methods. She is one of the rock stars in our field that I admire greatly.

Upon the arrival of coffee, Brett leans forward, elbows on the table, "Can I ask you a personal question, Taylor?"

A couple more stirs of the cream in my white China cup, "Sure. What's on your mind?"

"How are things going for you at home? Things between you and Jake?"

"Fine, I suppose. He's been putting in lots of additional hours with his new position, so he's preoccupied much of the time, but I hope that the summer will give him a break. It will be nice to spend some time together—maybe get away for a long weekend."

"So, Jake hasn't mentioned a conversation he and I had last week? Last Thursday?"

"Well, no," I reply. It is not unreasonable that they would cross paths on campus, then, teasingly I ask, "Did the conversation include me?"

Brett never takes his eyes off mine. "Look, we've been friends for a long time now. About thirteen or fourteen years?"

I nod, feeling my stomach begin to tighten. I have no idea where this is going, so I just listen.

"Look, this is hard for me, so I'm just going to share it. I was walking to the auditorium last Thursday afternoon for a full faculty meeting and I came upon a couple near the side door, so I turned and went in through the main entrance. I said hello to a few people then found a seat near the back of the room. You know, for a quick exit in case my beeper went off."

"A quick escape. Sure," I say.

"The couple I'd seen outside then came into the auditorium and sat in front of me, down two or three rows." Brett stops talking and takes a gulp of his coffee. "While the administrators boasted about another great fiscal year, the couple whispered, leaned into one another, held hands, and he even kissed her." Brett takes another drink of his coffee. "Taylor, the couple turned out to be Jake and Linda and I'm very sorry to be the one to tell you."

I fall back against the upholstered chair, my thoughts random and spinning in my head. *Jake and Linda? My Jake?*

I am stunned. If this is true, then what did this mean about our twelve years together? Lies? Deceit? What was I supposed to be feeling right now? The questions kept popping into my head as I sat stunned.

"When I confronted Jake after the meeting ended, I told him that I would tell you about what I'd seen if he didn't come clean first. It seems he chose not to confess about the affair. Maybe he didn't think I'd say anything." Brett took a minute before continuing. "You must be devastated, and I hate that I'm the one dumping this crap on you, but I couldn't live with the truth knowing that you didn't know."

Brett reaches out and takes my hand. The feel of his touch brings me back to the present. "Jake and Linda. I don't want to believe it."

For the next twenty minutes or so, the past dozen years of my life run through my mind like a slide show. During my life's review, I hear Brett's voice. I can see his mouth moving, and occasionally, I recognize individual words, and every few minutes or so, I nod or manage to grunt out a word or two to acknowledge I am still aware of where I am. Finally, I must leave. I must get outside for a breath of cleansing air before I pass out.

I look into Brett's eyes, "Well, I'm devastated of course, but I can't think of another person I'd want to deliver such a bad truth. I trust you very much and know that you'll keep this a private matter until I have the chance to talk with Jake. Right now, I need some fresh air and a walk to clear my head." I stand, feeling dazed and overwhelmed.

Brett also stands. "Okay. Please call tomorrow and tell me how you're doing. And if there is anything I can do—anything at all— don't hesitate to ask."

"Sure. Yes. Alright. Tomorrow." I make a beeline for the door and once outside, I take in a long deep breath of cool ocean air.

My perfect day has ended.

The short walk back to my office is a blur. I am so consumed with my thoughts about Jake and Linda that I have no awareness of anything around me. I don't hear the waves. I don't notice the children on the beach. My world is utterly silent until I unlock the door to my office; I reach my sanctuary just as the tears stream down my cheeks. I have about thirty minutes until my next scheduled client.

I allow myself to cry for several minutes before making the call I knew had to be made. Surprisingly, Jake answers on the second ring.

"Hi, it's me."

"Taylor? Are you okay?" Jake asks.

"I just had lunch with Brett. It seems we have something to talk about. Will you be home on time tonight?"

"Yes, of course. I'm so sorry, Taylor. I didn't know how to tell you. And it just happened."

"Affairs don't just happen, Jake. This was a choice, a choice you and Linda made. But I don't want to discuss it over the phone. I'll see you at the house."

"Okay, I'll see you in a few hours."

I hang up the phone before Jake can speak another word.

The Dovers

Before I am quite ready for my next client, I hear hushed voices coming from the waiting room. The Dovers are on time. I had been working with Darrick for only six weeks when it seemed appropriate to invite his wife to join us to address some marital issues. Today is my introduction to Caryn whom Darrick described on many occasions as a "nag."

Well, I think, let's get this started. I take a very deep breath to try to clear my mind before walking into the small outer room. I extend my hand and greet Darrick and then Caryn. "Please come in and have a seat." I gesture to the empty seats.

Once my clients are settled, I begin the session. I am probably more anxious to get through this appointment than any other I can remember, but I put all my effort into forgetting, if just for the next hour, the news that Brett delivered to me over lunch. My husband of twelve years is having an affair—an affair with my old friend. Deep breath. *Focus.*

"I'm glad you could join us, Caryn. As you know, I've met with Darrick a few times and he's shared things that he would like to work out with you. He also said that many of these things have been raised in conversations between the two of you, so I thought it might work best to have you both present to try and resolve these recurring issues. How does that sound to you?"

"It would be a relief to have some closure on these issues. Quite frankly, I'm tired of never resolving anything with Darrick." Caryn flushes and looks down at the coffee table before her.

"Let's see what we can accomplish, but this won't happen overnight and may take several sessions. Are you open to that?"

"Yes. Whatever it takes." Caryn looks up and attempts a smile. "Okay, so you've been married for twenty-one years. Right?" They nod in unison. "That's quite an accomplishment on its own, so we'll see if we can take it another twenty-one." A wandering thought passes through my brain, *Will Jake and I see twenty-one years together?*

"Darrick told me that you asked for a divorce unless he sought counseling. Caryn, do you want to tell me what you wanted him to address with me?"

She looks me straight in the eyes. "He's a compulsive liar, and he's having an affair." Caryn lets the statement settle for a few beats before continuing. "The affair is with the golf course. We don't do anything together anymore because he's always off on his own. I don't know what he's doing half the time and the other half is spent hitting damn golf balls. This isn't the relationship I thought I was getting when I said, 'I do.' I want a partner; someone to spend time with and enjoy my life with. He just wants to be by himself." She pauses. "Since he retired, I feel like I'm wasting my time. I can't trust what he tells me, and he doesn't want to be with me. What's the point?" Caryn looks back down and straightens the fabric of her skirt.

"I hear quite a bit of pain in your voice. You're feeling hurt because your expectations of marriage with Darrick are not being realized. Let's talk about how the two of you communicate with each other. How do you express yourselves, ask for what you want and need?"

Caryn speaks immediately, "I am open and honest with Darrick. I have always been blunt about my wants and needs, but now, he just ignores me. He makes a mental schedule of his week and won't alter anything for me or the kids. But I don't know what he has planned because he doesn't tell me." Caryn looks as though a new revelation comes to her mind and continues, "He keeps this small piece of paper in his pocket, folded in quarters with written notes. Twenty-one years and I've never read his secret pieces of paper. If I ask him to do something that isn't on his schedule, he tells me he already has plans.

He comes and goes as he pleases, usually without telling me where he's going or what he's doing. He's a recovering alcoholic so I know something about addictive behavior, but he is so secretive about his life that I don't feel like I even know him anymore. Maybe I never really did." And, without a pause, she continues. "And he lies to me. He lies to my face when I ask him about smoking or what he's been doing and with whom." Tears are welling in her eyes now. "Darrick, what are you thinking about while listening to Caryn?"

I glance at the clock on the wall behind them. *Focus.*

"I don't live a secret life. I like to play golf and I don't know what the big deal is. Why is that the end of our marriage?" He shrugs and looks briefly at Caryn then back to me.

"I heard her say several things. She is feeling left out of your life, lonely, and perhaps even betrayed. She describes you as a compulsive liar and we talked about that just a couple of weeks ago. You told me that it was sometimes easier for you to tell her what you think she wants to hear rather than the truth. Smoking has been a hot button for the two of you, right?" *Deep breath.*

"He tells me that he isn't smoking when I know for a fact that he is. I've seen him out puffing away and I've had friends tell me they've seen him. My god, he had a minor medical procedure a couple of months ago and when asked if he smoked, he told the nurse no!" Caryn threw her arms up then let them fall hard onto her lap. "When he is caught in the act, he pretends to be remorseful, but I know he's not going to change. Why do you lie about it?" She glares at him for a short time then looks back at me and shakes her head.

"Darrick, can you answer that question? If you are going to continue to smoke, why not tell Caryn that?"

"I only smoke occasionally. It's not every day. Maybe once a week or less."

"Then why tell Caryn you haven't been smoking when you have?"

"I don't know," Darrick says.

"There it is. His favorite response to everything, I don't know. He acts like an adolescent."

"Darrick, what do you think is going to happen if you just tell Caryn that you have smoked when she asks you?"

"I don't know. She's just going to start a fight."

Caryn is ready with a comment. "I asked you to stop smoking years ago for our health. This isn't something selfish I'm doing to control you, Darrick." Then Caryn looks at me. "I developed asthma some time ago and told him that he needed to quit smoking or to smoke outside the house away from me and the kids. You know second-hand smoke and all. I don't think I am being unreasonable."

"And what was your response to Caryn's request, Darrick?"

"'I said 'fine.' I had tried to quit many times before, so trying again was no big deal."

"And was it a 'big deal'?" I ask.

"Well, I didn't stop completely. But I'm not smoking around her, so what's the problem?"

Suddenly, Caryn spoke up, "Because you told me you had quit. You said you weren't smoking anymore. You see, when you tell me one thing and are really doing something else, it's lying."

"I thought you said that was 'passive aggressive'?" Darrick quipped.

I had to intervene at this point. "Okay. Time out. We're not going to resolve this today, but I have identified a few behaviors we can focus on to improve your interactions for now." I give them a moment to breathe and deflate their heightened emotions before I continue, "I'm not suggesting this is in any way a contributing factor to your struggles, but it's obvious that there is an age difference between you. Darrick, you may have even mentioned this during our first meeting, you are twelve years older than Caryn. Is that right?" God, twelve years of my life that may be thrown away because of Jake's affair. *Focus.*

"Yes. But it didn't seem to make any difference twenty years ago," Caryn added.

"How did you meet?"

"Mutual friends set us up on a blind date. It was awful for me, at least the first five hours or so. I swore I wouldn't go out with him again if he asked."

Darrick rolled his eyes but didn't contribute a word. "Why was it 'awful' for you?"

"We went to a party at our friend's home. Once there, Darrick disappeared outside with the guys. Every thirty minutes or so, he would reappear and check on my wine and say 'hi.' At about nine o'clock, he excused us from the party so we could go to a movie. The only conversation we'd had was during the fifteen-minute drive from my place to the party. The next day was Easter and I spent it with relatives. When my aunt asked about the date, I told her that he was the most boring man I'd ever met and there would not be a second date." Silence.

"But there was a second date. Right?" I asked.

"Eventually. Darrick called once a week for a month asking to go out again, but I kept turning him down until one night when he really opened up with me over the phone. I finally got a peek into the person buried under all his silence. We made plans for another date then we were practically inseparable after that. He was gone one full month on military training, but we married just four months after our second date."

"Sounds romantic and spontaneous. So, Darrick, are you still in the military?"

"No. Retired about four years ago."

"You pursued Caryn after the first date. What was it that attracted you to her?"

Darrick didn't speak right away, then said, "She was pretty, and funny, and smart." A reflective silence filled the space between the couple.

"Well, this is a good place to end today's session. I do have an assignment for both of you though. I want each of you to ask the other to do something, one thing during the next week. Something that is important to you. Caryn, what would you like to ask Darrick to do?"

Caryn was quick with her request. "Tell me goodbye when you leave home."

"Darrick?"

After several minutes of thinking, Darrick responded, "Don't talk on the phone so much when I am home."

"Those requests sound very reasonable to me. How do you feel about what the other has asked of you?"

"Sounds fine. I can do that," Caryn responded. "Me, too," Darrick said quietly.

"Great. Then we'll pick this up next week at this same time. I look forward to working with you both. We'll take small steps over the coming weeks and see where we go."

With that, the couple stood and thanked me for the time and said they'd work on their assignments.

My thoughts drifted to my next appointment: meeting Jake at home in just a couple of hours. How did I feel about learning of his affair? How will this affect our marriage? I didn't have those answers at the moment.

THE CONFRONTATION

I am home in the back yard tossing a ball to Cali when I notice Jake standing on the patio. He is still in his work clothes minus his shoes. With a beer in one hand, he meekly waves when our eyes meet. At the same time, Cali drops the ball she had just retrieved and dashes toward the house to greet Jake. As I gather the balls and Frisbee, the knot in my stomach clenches tighter. For a moment, I think I might be sick, but as I walk to the patio, the knot eases, but my limbs start shaking and a warm numbness passes over me.

"Hi, babe," Jake says with hesitance in the volume of his voice.

"Hi, Jake. How do you want to do this?" I take a deep breath to calm the anxiety overtaking me.

"I don't know. I never thought of this scenario. I never imagined I would have this conversation with you."

"And yet, you are. I assume you told Linda that I know about the two of you. She called my cell a couple of times while I was with clients, but she didn't leave messages." Jake nods and silence consumes the space between us. Cali bounces from one idle hand to the other until we settle into chairs on the patio. Cali takes this cue to lap up some water and lay in the cool grass under a nearby crabapple tree.

"How long has this been going on?" I ask. What I really want to ask was how long he has been a lying and cheating ass, but I know it won't accomplish anything. I need to keep my head so we can get through the next few hours.

"Awhile. About a year, I guess. God, I never wanted to hurt you. Do you believe me? I don't want anyone to be hurt by my actions."

"Well, that's naive and a little too late. I am devastated, Jake. I trusted you completely. And to have an affair with one of my closest friends? Or who I thought was a close friend. I feel deceived by both of you. This situation of yours has shattered the foundation of what I knew to be true in my life." I take a deep breath and look away to compose myself just as a tear runs down my cheek.

"Can you at least tell me why I had to learn about your affair from Brett? Didn't he say that he was going to tell me if you didn't? He's known for about a week, and you didn't say a word."

"I can't explain myself, Taylor. It just happened."

"Affairs don't just happen, Jake. They are choices that are made, selfish and very stupid choices." The anger began to bubble up from my core when Jake tried relinquishing responsibility.

"You're right, I know. I just can't explain why I did it. I love you; I do." He looks down and slowly shakes his head, as if in disbelief over what he has done or maybe that he's has been found out. Psychologically speaking, one could argue that his subconscious wanted the truth revealed because of his public behavior on campus. But what result did he favor? I don't believe he has a clue at this point. I certainly don't.

"Jake, if we had been having problems, I think I could understand you going outside our marriage, but there was no indication that you were unhappy or dissatisfied. I wasn't. So, I think it would be best for me if you move out of the house until we can sort through the truth and what we want for the future—together or not." It's as if a calming blanket had been laid over me; my mind became clear and I feel fairly objective, at least for the moment.

"You need to really look at the reason for your infidelity and I need to figure out how much damage you've done to my trust. I'm sure you can find a place to stay indefinitely. Can you make arrangements by the weekend?" I look at him with conflicting emotions—love and deep sadness.

"Of course, if that's what you really want. Can't we just talk this out? I won't see her anymore." Jake's voice sounds strained and desperate.

"Did you think there wouldn't be consequences for your actions? Did you really think you could trample all over my trust then find me with open and forgiving arms? That's outrageously unreasonable, Jake."

"No. You're right. You have every right to be angry. I know that I've hurt you and I'm sorry." I knew that his apology was sincere, but it was the intention behind the apology that bothered me. He had an opportunity to come clean about the affair himself but chose not to. In the end, he allowed someone else—a dear friend and colleague of mine—take on the burden of truth and I felt a deep disappointment in that. The incredible respect I had always held for Jake has taken a big hit with learning of his affair.

I have counseled possibly hundreds of couples struggling with issues resulting out of affairs, but I knew that the affair itself was just the result of other underlying problems within the relationships. I never thought I would be in this situation, surprised by the infidelity of my own husband when there had been no evidence of problems. Could I be so ignorant and disconnected to not see any sign at all? What will I learn about myself as we work through the process of climbing this hurdle in our relationship? Clearly, our individual needs were not being met as I had thought.

"Taylor, I know you're thinking that I was with Linda all the times I said I worked late or went into work early and that's not true. The promotion to department head really required more hours of me."

Somehow, Jake's confession did little to comfort me. But if he wanted to talk, I thought it would be good for me to hear him out.

"I guess it was convenience. We started just having lunch together when we'd run into one another at the cafeteria. Then we began coordinating times to meet for lunch. It was harmless, just friends and colleagues talking over lunch. But it became more around the time when my dad was diagnosed. Learning that he had a brain tumor really shook me up."

"I remember. The news was devastating for all of us," I interject.

"Maybe it was the thought of my own mortality, but I became worried that I hadn't lived enough or done enough with my life.

Linda was always checking in with me, asking how I was doing, how Dad was doing. Then, after his death, I felt . . . desperate and lost. You were so strong and never seemed to need anything. Anyway, about a month after we buried him, Linda stopped by my office on a Friday when most of the students and faculty had left and one thing led to another. I swear it wasn't planned. I don't even remember thinking about Linda that way before that day." Jake looked flushed and tired.

"When you say *that way*, you mean sexually. Right?" I don't want to feel sympathy for him at this point, so I focus on his most egregious act to deflect my feelings.

"Yes. I swore to myself each time we were together was the last. But, before I knew it, a year had passed. God, I'm so sorry, Taylor."

"I believe you, Jake. I'm just not sure what you're most sorry about: having the affair or getting caught. Either way, we have our work cut out for us."

With that, Jake looks at me, directly into my eyes and says, "I still love you. I understand why you think you can't trust me right now, but I hope you will again."

That night while Jake shuffles around the house, I spend an hour or so calling clients and canceling appointments for Friday. I know I will need time to reflect on my situation and prepare myself as best I can for what is to come, whatever that might be. It wouldn't be fair to my clients if I was distracted and unable to give them my complete attention.

Following my last phone call, I find myself sitting at the desk in my small home office staring at the pictures scattered around the room. A quote comes to mind. A quote I had read by a woman whose name I can't remember, *"The only thing that makes life possible is permanent, intolerable uncertainty: not knowing what comes next."* How absolutely true.

GOODBYE

As morning breaks on Saturday, I am filled with a deep sadness and longing to change the past. Silently, I wish that I hadn't learned the terrible truth about Jake's affair with Linda and this was just any other weekend in Chelsea. But it's not and my life has been changed forever.

After a lingering hot shower, I make my way to the kitchen for a bold cup of coffee. From the garden window, I can see Jake playing with Cali; tossing the ball across the yard then chasing after her to wrestle it back and continue the game. After a short while, I top off my mug then step out onto the deck. Cali dashes to greet me, out of breath and damp from the morning dew on the lawn. Jake follows slowly behind her.

The awkwardness between Jake and me and the abundance of raw emotions of the past few days have worn me out and my ability to concentrate on work has diminished. I find my mind wandering during conversations and while transcribing client notes, but my time spent talking with Brett has provided warm comfort. He has shown an interest in my well-being that goes beyond that of a colleague. We are friends. The additional support is welcomed because, I anticipate, the hardest part of the struggle is yet to come.

Jake has planned to stay in a friend's guest house on the beach during our separation and has packed his belongings and will be leaving this morning. My distress is coupled with a palpable anticipation to finally get past his leaving so I can move toward healing. I've made plans with Annette for dinner this evening, and if I know her at all, she'll insist on staying the night. I'm prepared with two bottles of Chardonnay and two romantic comedies for when I've tired of talking about my situation, my surprise, and my pain. She won't let me stew for long though; she'll have me up and back in yoga again in no time.

It is around ten in the morning when I watch Jake drive away. Cali is by my side tail wagging and letting out an occasional whimper. I fill the hours cleaning the house and reviewing notes in my client files. I find myself tending to the million small tasks that I've put off for months because of more important things. When I enter the guest bedroom where Jake has been sleeping, I begin to cry, softly at first until I drop on the empty bed and sob. The crying becomes uncontrollable and with so much intensity that it hurts; my temples begin throbbing, and my stomach is aching. Eventually, I drift off to sleep, exhausted. Cali is cuddled closely beside me to comfort her distraught master.

I awaken around three in the afternoon to a soft rain outside. Cali is restless and in need of a stretch and run around the back yard. I put on a CD to break the deafening quiet and putter around the kitchen preparing a dinner of salmon and steamed vegetables. For a real treat, and to help purge my lingering heartache, I have included a dessert of strawberries from a local farm that I've double-dipped in white chocolate—a truly sinful but delicious treat that I usually only allow myself on special occasions of celebration, but this most certainly will not be an evening of merriment.

Annette arrives shortly after six o'clock armed with a large bouquet of mixed brightly colored flowers and a hug that warms me deeply. I am reminded that I am not alone in my life, and she will always be here to support me.

Sitting on the deck as the sun slowly begins its descent, I fill Annette in on the nitty gritty details of my situation.

"I just can't believe Jake would do this . . . have an affair." Annette shakes her head and takes another sip of wine.

"He says it just happened and that really makes me angry. Like the lack of conscience is going to win him my forgiveness. And why Linda? We've been friends for years." Then to lighten the mood a bit, I ask, "You're not planning to seduce Jake, are you?"

We both let out soft laughter and raise our glasses to acknowledge the idiocy of the situation. For a few moments, we sit silently just taking in the beautiful sunset. My mind drifts to thoughts of what the future might hold for me until Cali nuzzles me back into the present. I fire up the grill and in no time, we are enjoying a delicious meal and lighter conversation.

Hours later, I awaken in my favorite chair in the living room; it is around four in the morning. The television is muted but lighting up the room, revealing Annette on the couch cuddled up with Cali and a blanket. Quietly, I get up and turn off the T.V. and take the glasses and empty wine bottle to the kitchen. A light flashing from my cell catches my eyes and when I check the voice mail, I see Brett left a message earlier in the evening.

"Hi, Taylor. I just wanted you to know that I was thinking of you and hoping your day was going better than anticipated. I'm glad you made plans with Annette and remember you can call me anytime. I'll talk to you later."

I press "nine" to save the message, not because I will forget that he called, but to replay it later to again feel the kindness envelope me. I return to my chair in the living room and sleep another few hours with my best friend nearby.

GABRIEL

After Cathie leaves the office, I greet Gabriel who is reading a sports magazine while waiting for his appointment.

"Hi, Gabriel. Please come in and get comfortable." I make note that his attire is like the shorts and t-shirt he wore previously. This time, the surf shop logo catches my eye. Something seems familiar about it.

"Pacific Crest. That's a different logo than the shirt you wore last time. Is this the name of your company?" I ask.

"Yeah. You've probably seen it around cuz we're local and all."

"Have you always used this logo? Something about the brand seems different to me."

"Wow, yes, Wes and I made minor changes to it after my first partner, um, well, took off."

Gabriel chooses a chair then suddenly appears uncomfortable.

"Your partner left you with the business?"

For a split second, my mind jumps to Jake's affair and how desperately unprepared I was for that news. A business partner walking away could have the same effect on a person.

"Actually, it was a major surprise. I mean, he just disappeared one day. C.J. brought Wes into the business just months before without talking it over with me and I was ticked about it, then he took off and that really pissed me off. C.J. and I were buddies from way back in elementary school. We got pretty tight and stayed that way even after he moved up here and started Pacific Crest. He talked me into coming up two years after he got it off the ground. He was good with the business side, and I knew surfing, so it worked out well. He did sales and I took over the custom shop."

Suddenly, like cold water had been dumped over me, I realize the connection and familiarity. Could it be?

"You call him 'C.J.,' what do those initials stand for?"

"Uh, Calvin James."

"Calvin James?" I am astonished and try hard not to alarm Gabriel of my connection to him and his wife, Annette.

"Yeah. You know him?" he asks somewhat surprised by my recognition.

"I am very close to his wife, Annette, and I certainly would call Calvin a friend."

My heart is racing just thinking of the possibility of tracking him down for my best friend's sake. Learning the truth behind his disappearance and finally getting some closure after five agonizing years would help Annette enormously.

"Do you know where he left to? Do you know what he's doing now?" I maintain a calm, inquisitive tone.

"You know, that's the thing, he never said. He just never showed up again. The police even came around a few times asking questions. I didn't know anything that could help them." Gabriel pauses for a moment, deep in thought, and then adds, "He really liked the ladies though."

I felt my stomach knot up recalling the many times Calvin cheated on Annette. She never walked out on him, never really talked of divorce. He'd apologize and take her somewhere for a long weekend and all was forgiven.

As intrigued and curious as I am about this connection, I remind myself that this is a therapy session to help Gabriel, so I need to focus on him now.

"Well, in relation to this event, when did your sleep problems start?"

Gabriel sits quietly for a short time, staring at the table and chewing on his thumbnail. "About five years ago, so it was really close; within a couple of weeks of C.J.'s disappearing act."

Many of us lost sleep during that time. Certainly, his old friend and business partner would have. "Did you keep the sleep journal that we discussed last week?" I ask.

"Oh, yeah. I did. I averaged waking five times during the night. Guess that's why I feel like I'm dragging in the mornings."

"Yep, most likely. Did you remember any of your dreams and to write them down?"

"Not entire dreams, just parts of them. I had one dream a couple of nights. All I can remember is I'm paddling my surfboard out from shore but there aren't any waves big enough to ride, so I keep paddling until I'm out in the middle of nowhere. I'm just sitting on my board in the middle of the ocean."

"Do you recall what you were feeling sitting on your board in the middle of the ocean?" I ask.

"I guess I was surprised."

"Surprised by what?"

"That there weren't any waves."

"Any other feelings like nervousness, anxiety, disappointment, or excitement?"

"I think I was a little nervous or maybe more confused being in the ocean by myself with just my surfboard. I felt pretty cool about things until I was in the middle of nowhere with nobody else around and no land in sight."

"Then what happens?"

"That's it every time."

"Why do you think there are no waves to catch? Have you ever gone surfing and not been able to because there weren't any waves?"

"Nah, never. I mean, there are days when the swells are calm but there are always waves."

"You know, dreams are subject to an array of interpretations but there's one belief that dreams can be prophetic and foretell the future, while other people believe that dreams are merely the brain's way of ridding itself of the rubbish from the day. Dream symbolism and dream interpretation are just one small aspect of dreaming."

I take out a piece of paper and begin writing as I talk of possible meanings of Gabriel's recurring dream. "An ocean in a dream can represent the context of your life, meaning where you're at and the situations taking place in your life. Or it can represent the unknown—a huge, deep area that holds secrets, maybe that vast ocean." I pause to collect my thoughts before continuing. "The sand is symbolic of the rational and mental processes, while the water signifies the irrational, unsteady, and emotional aspects of yourself."

I take a breath and assess Gabriel's interest. "To dream that you are looking at or for something or someone may imply that you need to take a much closer look at some situation or relationship. Perhaps, you need to approach a situation from another perspective or viewpoint. Alternatively, it may represent your passivity and your need to start taking action."

"In any case, in any interpretation, we will look deeper into how Calvin's or C.J.'s abrupt leaving affected you personally and the business. It will be a journey, like your dream."

Gabriel's eyes are transfixed on me, because either he is interested, or he is thinking I am out of my mind. "What are you thinking, Gabriel?"

"I don't know. I'm feeling a little uncomfortable. I thought you'd just tell me to meditate and take some pills to help me sleep. I didn't know all of this could be anything deeper."

"We'll just take one step at a time and see where you lead us. Did you note your activities on the days when you had this dream? Was there anything, any pattern that caught your attention?"

"Uh, I didn't really look at that."

"Do you have your notes with you?"

"Yeah. They're in my Jeep. I can bring them up to you," he offers.

"Yes. I would like to look at what you noted, who knows, there may be no pattern to your dream's occurrence, but let's see. Is there anything else you wanted to talk about today?"

"Nah. This is plenty for one day!"

"Okay. Keep journaling and we'll pick this up next week." We both stand and walk toward the door. Gabriel tells me he'll be right back with his notes then I copy the papers and slide them into his client file.

What a small world, I think. Calvin James—after all these years.

ABIGAIL

It feels like months have passed since I last saw Abigail; we will have much to talk about this morning. She is running late by my clock, but that is not unusual for my teenage client. After just a few more minutes, I hear the outer office door open, and she quietly enters.

As I approach her, I sense something is wrong. She looks beautiful as always and is dressed skimpily as is the fashion for teenagers these days, and Abigail still has on over-sized sunglasses but is wearing a soft brace on her left hand and wrist.

"My goodness," I stop in my tracks and stretch out my arms to her. "What happened to you?"

"Nothing serious, it was my fault. It's just a sprain." Abigail makes a beeline for the couch, deposits her keys and sunglasses on the coffee table, and takes a heavy seat.

"Do you want to tell me how you sprained your wrist?" I ask.

"I guess it looks worse than it is because of this thing." She lightly touches the cream-colored brace. "It'll be fine in another couple of weeks."

I wait a short time, but Abigail does not offer any explanation, so I move the conversation on.

"Graduation was a couple of weeks ago. How did everything go?"

"It turned out to be fun. My brother even showed up with Dad; it was nice to see him, even for just a few minutes. After the ceremony ended, we went to dinner then I went to a big party at the beach with all my friends. We stayed up all night talking, laughing, dancing, and even playing volleyball!" Her eyes are bright and the smile on her lovely face tells me that she really did have a good time.

"Did you give the commencement address?" I ask. Abigail had agreed to speak months earlier, but after her mother's suicide, she was having second thoughts. She even contemplated skipping out on the graduation ceremony altogether.

"Yes, I did. I decided to do it for my mom. It was a lot harder than I anticipated, but I got through it and was glad when it was over."

It touches my heart to see this young woman, wounded by the death of her mother, to take the necessary steps to heal the pain she is feeling so she can move forward with her life.

"I'll bet your dad was very proud of you."

With that, Abigail looks down and touches her injured wrist. "Yeah, I suppose," and quietly adds, "but that didn't last long."

"What do you mean by that?"

"Nothing. I know he was proud of my speech." When she looks back at me, tears have puddled in her eyes, but she fights them back by blinking several times.

"Abigail, how did you hurt your wrist?" The subtleness of her touching her wrist when mentioning her dad indicates to me that there is a story there and I want to hear it. "Our conversations are confidential. Remember?" Knowing that her dad is the Mayor of Chelsea complicates her frankness at times and it helps when I remind her that what she shares will stay between us.

"Like I said, it was my fault. I was sitting at his desk, just drinking some tea, and looking out the window when something caught my eye—a piece of paper in the color of my mom's stationary, so I pulled it out of the pile on dad's desk. The letter was in my mom's handwriting, and I saw her name at the bottom, but I didn't have time to read it because my dad appeared out of nowhere. The next thing I knew, he grabbed my hand and twisted it, so I'd drop the note. He didn't mean to hurt me, but he definitely didn't want me to read what she wrote." She squares her jaw and adds, "It was dated the day she died."

I'm surprised by her words and immediately wonder if Abigail's mother, Teena, had indeed left a suicide note.

"When did this happen? When did you find the note?"

"Yesterday, after church. Afterward, Dad went up to his room with the note, but just a few minutes later, I heard him leave and I haven't seen him since. I want to ask him what it says. I want to know if it explains my mom's suicide. You know, why she chose to kill herself. Does she mention me in the note? I just want to understand why she's gone. I miss her so much, but I'm mad, too. What happened to make her so unhappy? And now, what's it like for her?" Abigail looks into my eyes and asks, "Do you believe in heaven? Do you think people who commit suicide go there?"

"Those are exceedingly difficult, philosophical, and personal questions. I want to believe that there is a kind of paradise waiting for us beyond this life, one where it would take much more than an act of suicide to keep us out. The woman you've described and shared with me was a loving and spiritual person whose soul most certainly has found peace now." I let the silence settle before continuing.

"Abigail, do you think your father would join us for a session? Would you be comfortable with that?"

"Yeah, it'd be fine with me, but I doubt that he'd come."

"Do you mind if I invite him? I'd be happy to call and ask him to join us next week."

"It might be better coming from you. He might even squeeze in the time," she says with a tone of sarcasm and a shrug.

"I'll do that. I'll give your dad a call." I make a note on the yellow pad resting on my lap.

"What do you have planned for the rest of the week? Have you looked into yoga classes yet?"

"Absolutely. I was going to start going three times a week, but I'll have to wait till my wrist is better now. Geri is going to go with me." Suddenly, Abigail's face lights up and she adds, "Did I tell you that she's decided to go to Stanford too? We're gonna share an apartment, so that'll make the move easier for both of us."

"Well, that couldn't have worked out any better. I'm very happy that the transition is coming together for you. When do classes begin? Do you know when you'll make the move?"

Abigail is almost giddy at this point. "Classes start the first week of September, so we'll be moving up a week or two before. Dad knows someone, a friend in Palo Alto looking for a condo and making all the arrangements for us. We'll just drive up and move our stuff in. Geri's really excited about college, and I am getting more so now."

"Abigail, I know you don't feel it at times, but you have made tremendous progress over the past few months. I want you to recognize how far you've come and acknowledge how hard you've worked to get here. Despite the trauma of losing your mom, you stayed in school, graduated, and you're planning for college. That's a lot in six months. I'm immensely proud of you."

"I couldn't have done it without you, Taylor. You've been very supportive and kind. I have really appreciated the guidance and your patience with me." Abigail blushes and again, her eyes fill with tears.

"You have done all the work. I'll make the call to your dad and see what arrangements I can make with him before you leave town. Is there anything else you wanted to talk about today?"

"No, I'm going for a pedicure then meeting up with Trisha for lunch. You have a nice day, Taylor." Abigail is already on her feet with keys in hand and sunglasses on. I walk her to the door, give her a gentle hug, and she is on her way.

I return to my desk to check voice mail before making the call to the mayor's office to talk with Johnston. There are two messages from Jake asking for us to get together and talk about our separation. It's only been a few weeks since he moved out of the house, and I'm not ready to discuss the future yet. He has been anxious to "patch things up" and has been applying too much pressure for my comfort, which has resulted in my pulling back and resisting his requests to meet. He should have considered these consequences before starting his affair with Linda.

I'll talk to him from home tonight, I say aloud to myself and dial the mayor's private office number.

Once I have Johnston on the phone and relay to him how well my sessions with Abigail have been going, I ask if he would be amenable to joining us during her next session. I explain Abigail's need for understanding her mother's final act and that he may be able to offer insight that I couldn't possibly provide. He is quiet and reluctant then asks if we can first meet privately without Abigail. He has something to discuss before he shares it with his daughter.

"Of course, Johnston. Do you want to come in an hour before Abigail? If you choose to join us, you can simply stay for her appointment time." He agrees and I make the change to my schedule.

"I'll see you then, Johnston."

I think how my job is all about secrets. Why did I not have any inclination of Jake's secret affair? In ten years of practicing psychology, I feel disappointed that I was caught so unaware and off guard. *My life lessons*, I think to myself.

THE DOVERS

I approach the Dovers who are in the small reception area, seated opposite one another in total silence. It is Wednesday and I have just wrapped up my weekly call with Brett. Weeks have passed since he broke the truth to me of Jake's affair. My first session with both Darrick and Caryn to address marital problems followed that conversation. I anticipate that I, too, will be addressing some of my own issues of spousal trust and control while working with them. The timing is not lost on me as I invite them into my office.

Once they are seated, I ask how the previous week had been. Caryn is usually the first to speak, but today, it is Darrick who responds.

"It really seems like I can't do anything right for her. She says she wants one thing one day, and then she complains about something else the next. I can't keep up with what will make her happy," Darrick says with his hands tightly clenched in his lap.

"Darrick, would you share specifics with me?"

"She wants me to tell her everywhere I go, and then she gets mad when I tell her that I'm going to play golf. She wants me to be truthful about when I've smoked, but then she gets mad. I don't need to know every detail about what she's up to, so why is it so damned important to her? I don't care that she spends so much time with her friends, why can't she let me just enjoy the time I have with mine?" He is quiet for a moment as if waiting for Caryn to jump in to debate him, but she does not.

I make eye contact with Caryn after a short time. "Caryn, you are noticeably quiet this afternoon. Do you want to tell me what's on your mind? Do you want to respond to what Darrick has shared?"

Caryn contemplates her words before speaking. "Darrick and I have been politely following through with our weekly assignments, but it has been made very clear to me that I don't really know him and that he doesn't want me to know him. He didn't have the compulsion to be away from me in the early years of our relationship; we seemed to enjoy each other's company quite a bit. But I've realized that it was me who did all the talking and sharing; Darrick just listened—didn't really reveal much about himself, his dreams, or his goals. He's always been closed off. I guess what I'm trying to say is that I've been making assumptions for twenty-one years that we want the same things, but we don't. We don't with each other anyway." She looks in Darrick's direction but doesn't make eye contact then she calmly continues.

"I've thought a lot about us the past year. Actually, I can think of little else, and I really wanted things to be better—much better. I wanted to know Darrick and feel closer to him, but he has to want that, too." Caryn turns to Darrick and takes a deep breath.

"I just wanted to be included in your life, Darrick, so I followed after you left the house this morning." Darrick sat completely still, looking back at his wife.

"I honestly had no idea I'd learn what I did and I'm not angry, Darrick. Actually, I feel some relief." Darrick closes his eyes and lowers his head. Neither of them speaks as a calmness fills the room. I wait to hear what has been discovered.

Caryn looks back to me and adds, "I followed Darrick to a condominium complex on a golf course just north of the university. He's having an affair, Taylor. He's having an affair with another man."

I've been counseling individuals and couples for more than a decade; I thought I'd heard it all, but I did not anticipate her revelation. The accusation of him having an affair was raised by Caryn before but Darrick isn't denying it this time.

"Darrick, are you okay?" He is still, sitting with his face in his hands. Slowly, he sits up, his back hard against the sofa.

"I don't know what to say. I can't say that it's not true because, obviously, she's seen us. Part of me feels . . . relieved, I guess."

"How long have you known you were gay, Darrick?" I ask.

"It's such a cliché, but I'm sure I've always known. I think I'm bi-sexual because I always enjoyed being with Caryn and the other women before her. Thomas is the first man I've ever been with, and I want to feel really bad about it, but I don't." Darrick looks toward Caryn. "I didn't mean to hurt you. I never wanted you to even know about my exploring a relationship outside of our marriage."

"Yes, well, that makes me feel so much better, Darrick," Caryn says, the tone spewing with sarcasm. "I feel some relief just knowing the truth; knowing now that it wasn't my imagination. And to be honest, sex was never an issue; I mean it was always good for both of us when we had sex. I'm most concerned about the kids and how they're going to react."

Darrick's eyes widen and his face reddens. "The kids? Why are we telling the kids? Why do they need to know? I don't even know where this is headed or if it's right for me."

"Because they're teenagers and we're all so very tired of your lies and half-truths. Aren't you tired of living a lie? Aren't you exhausted hiding your real self? We'll never move forward until we get all of this out in the open. I can't live this way any longer." Caryn's shoulders drop then she looks to me for support.

"You certainly do have decisions to make, and you have options as to how you figure this all out. The first is that of continuing therapy. Other important matters to discuss are how and when to let your kids in on the situation, and, of course, your living arrangement."

"Well, I definitely need some space and I don't care if you stay or go. Either way, we'll have to tell the kids something. They're teenagers, they'll ask questions." Caryn is clearly avoiding eye contact with Darrick and speaking directly to me.

"I'm not ready to make any changes right now." Darrick says.

A wave of empathy washes over me as my mind replays Jake leaving our home so recently. It was the right decision for us, but this couple will need to come to their own conclusion of what is best for them and their teenagers. Research of the past several decades examining the effects of divorce on children have been enlightening and spotlight the potential for increased depression and anxiety, as well as more outwardly signs of difficulty coping like acting out, delinquency, and impulse problems. I will discuss with the Dovers in future sessions.

For just a moment, I feel thankful that Jake and I do not have children to drag through our own current and messy situation.

"My recommendation is to table the family discussion for now and focus on adjusting to the revelation for you, Caryn, and determining where this relationship might be heading for you, Darrick. There are so many other lives entangled in this that everyone will need to be accounted for. Firstly, you need to take care of yourselves. Can you agree to taking time for a couple of weeks? If the kids suspect something is up, they'll let you know. Am I right?"

Caryn is now perched on the edge of the couch cushion and agrees to keep the talks between the two of them for now. Darrick just nods.

I think how I wouldn't want to be in their shoes for anything as they leave my office.

Several weeks have passed since learning of Jake's affair with Linda. Having avoided talking to Linda about the situation, perhaps I am wishing it away. Being betrayed by a good friend hurts as badly as knowing it was with my husband. I know that someday I will have to confront Linda, but not just yet.

It's Wednesday, but I'm not following my usual routine at this hour. I normally would be on the phone or meeting with Brett to discuss my caseload or my personal situation, which has become a regular topic for us. He is comfortable to talk to and is careful not to offer up his biases or opinions. He simply reiterates his trust that I will do the right thing for me.

The rain is coming down hard from a gray and ominous sky as I drive up the coast. Did it know something about my impending meeting with Jake? We had agreed to meet with a therapist outside of Chelsea, a woman I had met at conferences and read about in trade papers. Roz Shepard had a reputation for being one of the most talented therapists in the country. She has trained with the most prominent names in our field and practices the most progressive therapeutic methods in our area. Brett and Roz are well-acquainted and team up regularly to provide weekend workshops for couples or individuals desiring an intense therapeutic experience. It was with Brett's influence that I was able to schedule time with Roz, circumventing the average three-month wait.

I make my way along the winding road from the highway and my anxiety begins creeping into the pit of my stomach. My thoughts of reconciling or not with Jake vacillate with the curves of the road. I know that my future is of my own making, and I am not about to rush into any decision that might be detrimental to my happiness.

My heart is bruised and my trust in Jake shattered by his affair. I snap back to the present when I reach the road's end; the view is spectacular.

Perched on a high bluff is Roz's complex where she practices. It is a substantial building of logs and glass with a panoramic view of the ocean and cliffs settling at the water's edge far below. The feeling and presentation are that of an upscale resort, absent any clues of its intended and primary purposes: counseling and healing.

To the right is a small cluster of two-story apartments not unlike the main building in their construction. Three structures are set end to end creating a triangular garden in the center. *Lodging for her weekend workshops*, I whisper. Beautiful and convenient.

I park my Prius in front of the main building just as my attention is drawn to the SUV that has appeared beside me. It is Jake and he nods slightly and smiles—tenuous greetings and an awkward hug before making our way up the steps to the door.

Inside the building, Jake and I are greeted by a friendly young woman. "I'm Tracy. Please follow me and I'll get you settled in. Roz will join you shortly." A walk down a short hallway leads us to one of three heavy postured doors. We follow Tracy through the only open door, entering a room flooded with natural light.

The room offers floors in rich mahogany, six inviting upholstered chairs, and a stacked rock fireplace that rises from floor to ceiling on one wall. But the scene-stealer is the expanse of windows framing the ocean outside. The twinge of anxiety I was feeling about this appointment with Jake dissipates as I take in the impressive view.

"Can I get either of you something to drink?" I hear Tracy's voice. "We have just about anything you might fancy. Water, coffee, colas." For the first time, I hear just a tease of an English accent.

"I would love water, Tracy. Thank you," I say. Jake shakes his head and mouths the word "nothing." In just seconds, she reappears with a glass of water and places it on the table beside my chair. "Roz will be right in. It was my pleasure meeting you." Then Tracy is gone again. Jake and I meet eyes once more with raised eyebrows. I am impressed so far and hopeful it will translate to Roz as well.

As though reading my mind, a tall, slender woman appears in the doorway, closing it quietly before she turns to us. I recognize Roz immediately. "Good afternoon," she says as she extends her hand to Jake who is closest to her. "Hello, Jake, I'm Roz Shepard." Then she walks to me, "Taylor, it's a pleasure to see you again." After greetings are made, we sit and await Roz's lead.

"As I understand from Brett, the two of you have encountered a situation in your marriage. Is that correct?" Roz looks up from the open file folder now lying on her lap.

"Yes, that's right," I say. Jake sits quietly but nods in agreement. "I became aware that Jake was having an affair with one of my friends several weeks ago. We've been separated since then and are here now to talk about how we got to this place." The matter-of-fact tone of my voice surprises me and Jake as well by the look he shoots my way.

"Okay. Jake, can you tell me about the relationship Taylor is referring to?" Roz asks.

"Linda is both a friend and colleague. We've known one another for many years, but only developed a closer relationship about a year ago," Jake says quietly.

"What do you mean by 'closer'?" Roz queries.

"Physical," Jake replies then looks down to avoid eye contact.

Roz continues, "Were there difficulties between the two of you prior to or around the time the affair began? Was there something that occurred to affect your relationship?"

Jake looks at me before responding. "My father became terribly ill and then passed. I suppose that was when I first felt isolated and withdrawn from Taylor. I don't know why, but I didn't talk about it much with her. Linda showed a great deal of concern and so we began spending more time together. We didn't become physical for quite some time though." Jake looks at me and then continues, "That didn't happen until months later. Taylor was incredibly supportive during my dad's ordeal and didn't deserve this." Jake hangs his head and shakes it gently back and forth.

I look to Roz, thinking how dramatic and insincere Jake seems, a side of him I had not seen before. I think how pathetic he is coming across.

"Well, we're not here to point fingers and place blame. Our goal is to figure out what fractured your relationship; what went askew for you to seek out another woman's affection," Roz says, alternating her eye contact between the two of us.

Roz looks to me, "Taylor, do you recall Jake pulling away and isolating during the time he's mentioned? Do you remember a change in Jake's behavior during his father's illness?"

"I recognized his grief and I thought we were engaged and talking through it. It was a stressful and dreadful time. Much of our attention was focused on his mom and giving her additional support." I take a breath. "It's not uncommon for Jake to become introspective and shut me out for short periods of time, so I had no clue that he needed more from me then."

"Is this the first time either of you has sought out another partner during your marriage?" Roz asks without directing the question to either of us specifically.

I am uncomfortably aware of Jake's unresponsiveness and look to him for an acknowledgment to the question.

"I know that honesty is needed at this point for us to move forward, so I have to admit that there have been other brief encounters prior to Linda." Jake's face flushes and he bites his bottom lip, avoiding my stare.

I'm in shock and feel dumbfounded and foolish for not seeing any signs of his infidelities. How could I have been so disconnected? So out of touch? A quick mental review of the last twelve years and still, I can't recall behaviors on Jake's part that should have triggered my suspicions. Our level of intimacy only waned with his current promotion, but we had even discussed the immediate effects it might have on our time together. I had always trusted Jake, maybe too much. I'm simply shocked.

The remaining time with Roz could not pass quickly enough for me after Jake's confession of numerous affairs throughout our marriage. A heavy weight settles on my chest, making breathing difficult and I become desperate for fresh air just beyond the confines of this office. I'm struggling to concentrate and stay engaged in the conversation going on around me. To be honest, I want to scream out loud until the aching of my heart eases, but I refuse to fall apart in front of the man who has deceived me for so many years. I know now that I cannot trust him again.

"Taylor, what's going on with you? You've heard some admissions from Jake that certainly are hard to learn. What do you want to say at this time?" Then, there was silence.

What did I want to say? What could I say? I just learned that my husband of twelve years has been unfaithful with many women who seemingly meant little to him. The shock I am feeling has been replaced with . . . nothing. I've become numb.

"I know that couples work through similar situations, but honestly, I don't think now that I have the desire to put forth the effort it'll take to reconcile with Jake. My mind keeps reviewing the past decade and I'm wondering now what it really meant; all the years that I will never get back. I'm also thinking that I am no longer interested in couples' sessions, but I will continue individually."

Continuing, I look at Jake. "I'm so disappointed and sad. If infidelity is your way of showing love, then I don't want yours. If you have a sex addiction, I want you to get treatment, but I am not going to sit quietly by waiting for you, Jake. You've shattered the trust I had for you; I have to take care of myself and do what's right for me."

At the end of the session, I made a series of follow-up appointments with Roz, then I had to get as far from Jake as possible. I didn't know where I would go from here, but it will be to a place I feel safe.

Within thirty-minutes, I am walking into Brett's office, hoping he is here and available to talk. The very moment our eyes meet, I know I am in the best place at this moment. Tears stream down my cheeks and I realize they are tears of relief, not grief. Brett walks to me and wraps me in his arms.

"You're okay," he whispers and holds me for quite some time.

THE KISS

While I pace the floor of Brett's office, I recount the conversation in Roz's office of the many affairs had by Jake. My loving husband turns out to be a scoundrel—a dirty, rotten, womanizing sex maniac and I never had a clue. "Can you imagine?" I ask without allowing Brett to answer.

Rambling on, "It's one thing when it was only Linda, but to learn that he had affairs throughout our entire marriage is surreal and, frankly, unforgivable. I will never be able to let this go and stay with him. My trust is shattered. It's gone. History. No question in my mind or my heart. My marriage is over." I finally sit.

After nearly an hour of rehashing every word and emotion shared during our session with Roz, Brett asks one simple question, "When are you going to get angry?"

Angry? I thought I was showing anger, but perhaps, I was so accustomed to staying in control for my clients that I hadn't really let go. Could I possibly just open my mouth, take a deep breath, and scream out? Allow the emotion to rise so I can discharge the disgust I feel? Telling Jake how hurt I was over learning of his affair with Linda, followed by his admission of many others certainly warranted anger, didn't it? I tell myself that I can use the energy from my anger of this betrayal to act and propel me forward, to heal and eventually trust again.

"You're right, of course." Looking into Brett's eyes, for the first time seeing his compassion, I realize how much I truly admire this man. And, for the first time, becoming aware of the attraction I feel as well. My heart skips then flutters deep in my chest. I feel myself melting into the gaze of Brett's chocolate brown eyes. I want to run my fingers through the locks of his soft brown curls and yearn to hold his muscular body to me once again, but this time, with new awareness of my feelings.

"Taylor, are you going to answer that? Where did you go? Your phone is ringing."

Shaking my head gently, "Oh, I didn't hear it." A glance at the number and I recognize it as Annette's.

"Hello?" It takes me a moment to release the fantasy I was having about Brett to comprehend Annette's words, "Calvin has been found." After five years, her absent husband has resurfaced. The police contacted her after talking with a psychiatrist in Oregon who disclosed that Mr. James had been under her care for two years and had just recently experienced a significant recall of memories while under hypnosis.

"I know you're going through a lot right now," Annette continues, "but would you feel up to coming with me to see him?"

"Of course, I'll go with you. Where is he now? Will his psychiatrist be with him?"

"I think that's what the detective said. Honestly, I didn't hear much past 'Calvin resurfaced in Oregon.' I'm closing the store. Pick me up?"

"I'll be there in thirty-minutes."

The moment with Brett is suddenly gone and disappointment washes over me and in its place is curiosity and anxiety to hear Calvin's story. How will he explain being gone for five years without any communication? A psychiatrist and hypnosis? What is this about?

"Annette's husband, Calvin, is alive and was living in Oregon."

Brett's eyebrows rise, "Geez, that'll be a story worth hearing."

"I've got to run . . . picking her up at the store." I stop at the door just long enough to mutter, *wow, lives are changing.*

Brett steps toward me and gently cups my face in his hands. "I hope you don't mind," then he leans in and kisses me so gently on the mouth that it takes my breath away. "Call me later when you can talk."

"Okay." In slow motion, I turn and walk through the office door, then look back at the gorgeous face watching me. "That was really nice, Brett."

I relive that kiss repeatedly in my head while walking to my car and once inside, I touch my lips and sigh.

Calvin Is Back

Before I know it, I am parked out front of the Four Seasons Boutique where Annette is pacing. Losing no time at all, she is buckling up in the passenger seat; she is pale, like she's seen a ghost.

"What are you feeling, Annette?"

"I feel pretty damn numb actually. For years, I wondered what this moment would be like. How would I hear the news? Where would I be? I always thought the voice on the phone would tell me where Calvin's body was found. The fact that he is still alive and never called or sent a letter really confuses me. And a psychiatrist?" Annette sits silently just shaking her head as if the motion would somehow make a difference.

"It's a shock, that's for sure. Remember, you are not alone." I place my hand on her arm for reassurance.

"You know, I never really believed Calvin was dead, but I gotta tell you, I'm shocked to hear it . . . to have confirmation that's he alive. I've created a whole new life for myself. Honestly, I think I had convinced myself that he left me to be with some other woman, and now, five years later, he's showing his face again with a shrink in tow, no offense intended. But I can't wait to learn what this is all about. Do you think he went crazy? Or do you think he has fabricated some unbelievable tale just to slip back into his old life? This whole scenario is so Calvin."

I think about Gabriel and wonder if he knows of this development. His long-lost partner comes out of the shadows to re-claim his life and business. Maybe Gabriel's dream of sitting idle on a surfboard in the middle of the ocean was a premonition. Maybe he was experiencing the calm before the storm.

I pull into the first empty space in the guest parking lot adjacent to the police station. Annette and I meet glances, then I say, "Remember to follow your instincts, and listen to your inner voice. You only need to take care of yourself and tell me what you need when you know." I smile and squeeze her hand.

Once inside the small police station, we find ourselves amid hurried commotion by uniformed officers and badge-wearing detectives. It's unclear to me if they are coming or going, but each undoubtedly has marching orders and places to be.

Suddenly, a voice from behind the front counter calls, "Annette." A waving hand garners our attention. "Annette, I can help you down here." With that, half of the officers stop, and the room goes quiet. Their attention is now focused on my dearest friend, who in her bewildered state, doesn't even notice the chaos cease upon hearing her name.

Ruthie Morris was one of the detectives who worked the case when Calvin was first reported missing by Annette so many years ago. Now, under seemingly bizarre circumstances, she will be stamping the file "closed" and moving it off her desk.

"You're looking pretty damned good considering everything," Detective Morris says as she places a hand on Annette's shoulder. "Let's get you into a quieter room in the back." With that, she glances my way and pauses.

"I can wait here if Annette prefers," I say anticipating Ruthie's question.

"No, I need you with me. Don't leave my side," Annette pleads.

Detective Morris nods and I follow them down a long sterile hallway of white walls lined with certificates, accommodations, and police portraits. We must pass half a dozen closed doors before reaching Ruthie's destination, a black door with a plastic placard engraved "Interview Room 4."

I enter the interview room behind Annette and Detective Morris. Looking around, I conclude it has remained unaltered in the five years since I last came with Annette to file the missing person report on Calvin. This time though, the emotions are of anxiety and anticipation instead of fear.

Once inside the room, Detective Morris motions for us to take seats then offers us beverages of our choice. Too nervous and curious, we both decline.

"What is going to happen now? How does this work?" Annette queries.

"Obviously, there is legal red-tape because of the missing person status and subsequent investigation five years ago. However, with the psychiatrist's statement, we may be in a position to just close the case as being resolved." Morris takes a breath then sits down next to Annette.

"Mr. James' explanation for his disappearance is that he got into a scuffle with at least one other gentleman behind a bar just across the state line in Spencer, Oregon. He claims he was struck with an object about his head that rendered him unconscious. Apparently, his identification and money were taken some time after the altercation. He was found later that evening when an employee of the establishment was taking trash to the dumpster. It has been substantiated that Mr. James remained in a coma for several days before awakening with extensive memory loss. He remained hospitalized for approximately one week during which time a nurse took an interest in Mr. James' situation and arranged for him to stay with her until he figured out what he was going to do. It seems that Mr. James did not make progress in regaining his memory on his own, so he worked odd jobs and over time, he simply settled into the community. About a year ago, Mr. James sought the help of Dr. Lampert for memory recovery. I'm told that he was able to recall some details of his life while undergoing hypnosis therapy with the doctor. This happened over time and multiple sessions. The most recent was Monday afternoon. Dr. Lampert contacted local law enforcement who then connected Mr. James to our open case, which brings us to this moment."

"I always imagined him living with another woman somewhere, but I couldn't understand him walking away from Pacific Crest. That business meant so much to him." Annette pauses and then quietly asks, "When can I see him?"

"Well, the good news is that he remembers you, the fact that you are married, and he wants to reconcile the relationship, if that's possible. If you are prepared, I'll bring him in so the two of you can talk on neutral and safe turf."

Nodding, Annette states clearly, "I'm ready." She takes my hand and holds it tightly.

Calvin

As the door closes behind Detective Ruthie Morris, my cell phone begins vibrating. I look at the number displayed. "It's my service," I tell Annette.

"You need to take the call. It'll be a while before they bring in Calvin." Annette nods and motions with both hands to answer the phone.

Not wanting to be a distraction, I walk to a corner of the room and in a quiet tone, accept the call. "This is Taylor Calloway."

The voice on the other end was familiar, polite, and professional. "Good afternoon, Ms. Calloway, Peggy with your service. I received a call from a client of yours, a Mr. Gabriel Hennessey. He asked if you would call him at your earliest convenience. I can text the number to you if you like."

"Yes, please text the number, Peggy. Is there anything else or is that all for now?"

"I took one other message from a 'Johnston' who called to confirm his appointment with you in the morning. No need to call him back unless there is a change. Others just left voice messages for you on your office phone—nothing urgent."

"Thank you, Peggy. I'll watch for the text and call Mr. Hennessey back." I disconnect from the call and immediately, a red light flashes consecutively with a vibration. I press a couple of buttons then hear the line ring out.

"Hello?" The man's voice is uneven, nervous.

"May I speak with Gabriel, please?"

Without a breath, he says, "Hey, Taylor." Gabriel sounds anxious and jumpy unlike the cool man that has been sitting in my office once a week the past month or so.

"What can I do for you?" I ask in a calm voice hoping to ease some of the nervous energy buzzing through the connection.

"Damn, did you hear? C.J. is back. I got a call from the police telling me he'd been in Oregon all this time with amnesia. Can you believe that? Amnesia. I don't know when I'm going to see him, but I just can't wrap my mind around this."

I look at Annette sitting at the gray metal table in the center of this cold and sterile room. "Yes, I did hear something about that. Do you want to meet me at my office at around six o'clock? We can talk about how this news is affecting you and how to handle the events to come."

"Yeah, six o'clock would be great. Thanks a lot. I'll be there. Whew." Gabriel lets out an audible sigh. "I'll see you then, Taylor."

"Try going for a walk or meditate to calm your nerves if you can. It might help to take the edge off until then."

"I'll try a walk and hope that helps. Thanks, I'll see you later."

On cue, the door opens and there appears a face seemingly unchanged by the past five years.

"Calvin," Annette says in a half-whisper carried across the room by visible relief at seeing her husband again. She stands but does not approach him. Sensing her emotional turmoil, I walk to the table and stand nearby waiting for the next words to be spoken.

Calvin never takes his gaze off Annette as he enters the room and walks to the table, stopping on the opposite side from her. He is waiting on her, following her lead as he was most certainly advised by his psychiatrist, who I assume to be the woman following closely behind. Once Detective Morris closes the door, Annette breaks the eye-lock with Calvin and we all take seats around the table, except for Detective Morris who remains standing by the door.

The woman sitting beside Calvin extends her hand to Annette, "Hello, I am Dr. Marcie Lampert and I've been helping Calvin the past year to find himself."

Calvin leans forward. "You look great, Annette."

"Yeah, and you look very much alive to me. I waited to hear from you for over three years before moving on with my life. At first, it was dreadful—a recurring nightmare. Eventually though, the cloud lifted, and I accepted you were gone, out of my life for the rest of my days on this earth." The look on Annette's face told all of us that she wasn't finished talking yet. "During our marriage, you could be a true bastard, Calvin, but still, I grieved for you. Turns out you had just gotten into another bad situation, and you paid a big price this time. You never thought of anyone but yourself then and now you're sitting here expecting me to believe some story about amnesia. It's very surreal."

Calvin nods. "I understand how far-fetched this sounds and I do not expect you to let me back into your life right away. I only hope you will give me a chance to make things right with you." He extends his hand out on the table and waits a short time before retreating when Annette does not reach back. "I always loved you, Annette. I know that I didn't show it well, but I want to make up for the time I've been gone and before when I was just an ass."

For the next hour, we listen to the details of the bar fight that caused the head injury and resulting memory loss. Dr. Lampert explains to Annette the exercises and techniques used that failed to recover Calvin's mental history until he agreed to hypnosis and regressive efforts. This resulted in high-percentage memory retrieval. She presents copies of police reports and session notes that Calvin agreed to share to help Annette reconcile his disappearance and explanation for so many years.

Calvin tries repeatedly to assure Annette that he had no recollection of their relationship at the time, or he would have returned immediately. "I've never wanted out of our marriage, that I can recall. I can feel it inside of me and I'll do whatever it takes to convince you this is where I want to be." He pleads.

Once Annette is satisfied with Calvin and Dr. Lampert's accounting of the events, she agrees to go to dinner with Calvin to talk in a more relaxed atmosphere. We all separate in the parking lot; Dr. Lampert is on her way back to Oregon, Calvin and Annette are going to The Cliff's restaurant near the beach, and I am heading back to my office in downtown Chelsea. I give Annette a supportive hug and remind her to call me later that night if she wants to talk about things.

It is nearly five-thirty, leaving me just enough time to get across town where a confused, anxious, and excited Gabriel will no doubt be waiting. Hearing the news of his good friend's resurrection has understandably knocked him off balance and in need of some therapy time with me.

GABRIEL

I am in my office just long enough to recall the tender kiss that made me swoon just before the commotion of Calvin's return to Chelsea. I close my eyes and relive the sensation of his hands on my face while his soft lips met mine, warm and electric. I think how nice it would have been to return the gesture with more time to savor the moment.

Suddenly, the outer door opens, jolting me back to reality. "Gabriel? Come on in."

Gabriel appears in the doorway. "Hi, Taylor. Thanks again for making time for me." He sits in his usual spot on the sofa then drops his keys and sunglasses on the coffee table. "Can you believe that C.J. is back?"

Actually, no, I think. "Let me share with you what I know, Gabriel. I just left the police station where I saw and talked with both Calvin and his psychiatrist. He looks very well and genuinely wants to pick up his life in Chelsea where he left it some five years ago." I pause to watch Gabriel's expression; he nods slowly.

"He was at a bar just across the state line when he found himself in a bad situation. He was struck in the head by an object that left him in a coma for a short time. When he regained consciousness, he had no memory of his life. His wallet had been taken, his keys and truck stolen, leaving him with nothing to connect him to any place or person until recently submitting to hypnosis that revealed enough details and memories to help his doctor and the police identify him."

"That's it? It sounds too simple, too clean," Gabriel said.

"I'm afraid that is the explanation for his disappearance. What do you think of going back into business with him? I believe he still wants to resume his place in Pacific Crest."

"I guess that's fine. I want to talk to him first cuz we've made changes and removed his name after he was gone about three years. But, sure, if this is legit, then he can get back in. I mean, Pacific Crest was his to begin with. It's just weird. It feels like life stopped or slowed down for five years, now the gears are kicking in again and time is moving forward."

I nod. "Imagine waking up one day with no recollection of the simplest of information like your name, birthday, address, who your friends are. Calvin had a wedding ring on but hadn't the slightest memory of his wife's name or face. Nothing. A blank slate. No doubt he experienced many times of extreme frustration over losing his data bank of history. Not all his memories have returned, and that's not uncommon. The important thing is that they are resurfacing, and he wants to re-engage with the people he knows, and he cares about."

Shaking his head, "I just can't imagine that happening. I bet he's scared. I would be. How's his wife doing?"

"Annette? She's a trooper and has lots of supportive people in this town and that'll get her through these next steps with Calvin, er C.J., as they figure out life with him back in it."

Gabriel stands and walks to the window looking out to the darkness that is the ocean. "I tried calling Wes on my way here. He didn't answer. When I told him this afternoon that C.J. was back, he looked shocked and sounded sort of puzzled by it. I remember thinking, *why would he be confused?* Then I thought that I really don't know the story behind Wes's connection to C.J."

Gabriel turns to me with a perplexed expression, "That's weird, right? Why don't I know that? We never talked about it after C.J. was gone; we just fell into a rhythm with the business. He had good ideas for improving the performance of the boards and I included the ideas into my custom jobs. We've done really well with the shop and growing our clientele. I wonder how that'll effect business having the founder back."

"You've worked hard, and you might want to keep that in mind when you do talk to Calvin about his return. Consider your stake in the business now that you've taken on the responsibility, success, and the ownership. Don't sell yourself short, Gabriel. If you think Calvin needs to earn his spot, then talk that out and make a plan."

I sit back and consider Gabriel's questions about Wes before responding. "As for Wes, what does your gut tell you about him? You've worked side-by-side for several years now, so you may not have asked specifically about his past, but you know some things about him. What are you really questioning about him now?"

"I think the timing of it all. Wes joined then C.J. disappeared within just a few months. I'm probably just overthinking things, but since the call from the police, my mind's been racing. I'm wondering what's real, what isn't. You know?"

"That is curious, but what concerns you most about the timing? Do you think there is a connection between the two things? Most likely, it's just coincidence." At least, I hope. "I mean, how could Wes be involved with C.J.'s disappearance in Oregon? That's probably taking a leap, don't you think?"

"When you put it like that, yeah. But there has been something nagging me in the back of my head all day. Wes acted squirrelly when I told him that C.J. was back and now I can't reach him. I'm sure it's paranoia or feeling overwhelmed by the changes coming. Maybe Wes just feels uncertain about his role now. Who knows?" Gabriel returns to the couch and sits deep in thought.

"Maybe it is. May not. Either way, you'll have to determine that, Gabriel."

For the next half hour, we talk about the business structure and what he'd like it to be then confirm our next meeting time before my client leaves the building.

It's all very curious indeed, I think.

JOHNSTON

Morning comes early after such an eventful evening. A revealing session with Jake, followed by a kiss from Brett, and then Calvin returning to Chelsea. But I'm back in my office ready to start my day and after checking voice messages, I see Johnston's figure in the doorway.

"Good morning, Johnston. Please come in and make yourself comfortable." I motion to the available seating in the room.

"Hello, Taylor. It's good to see you again." He walks right to me and extends his hand. "I'm here but I haven't felt comfortable anywhere since Teena's death."

"I'm deeply sorry, Johnston. Can I get you coffee or water?"

Johnston waves off my offer and eases himself into the chair positioned just across from the sofa where his daughter, Abigail, always sits and may be joining us in an hour.

Since Teena's death, the mayor and his daughter have grown desperately apart from one another because of Abigail's suspicion that her father knows more about her mother's reasons for taking her own life than he will share, and it's this notion that has driven a wedge between the two. Johnston agreed to sit with me and share what he does know, then he'll decide whether to stay for my next session with Abigail.

"Again, I appreciate you agreeing to meet and discuss Abigail's ongoing despair over Teena's suicide. She believes that you have insight shedding light on Teena's state of mind at the time of her suicide and that could bring understanding and healing for her."

Johnston never looks away from me but pauses before saying, "Teena was unhappy and left a letter for me detailing the anguish of her last year." The mayor takes a deep breath then continues, "I was unfaithful in our marriage. It's a cliché, but it happened. When Teena suspected the relationship, she confronted me and asked me to end it. I did, for a short time. I fell back into the relationship about six months before Teena died. She knew it then, couldn't sleep without medication, and she began drinking. She combined the two on the day of her death."

"Teena committed suicide because she didn't know how to deal with your infidelity. She intentionally killed herself. Is that what you're saying?" It seems that Johnston is avoiding the reality of Teena's act by referring to it as "her death" and not a suicide.

"We married young. I am with people every day. It was inevitable that I would meet other attractive women. I never intentionally went looking for someone else, but it happened, and I am paying dearly for my actions, but I never stopped loving Teena."

"I do understand that this is uncomfortable for you to share with me, but why not just come clean with Abigail so she can move on with her recovery? Are you afraid that she'll be angry and blame you for Teena's suicide?"

Silence. For several minutes in his quiet contemplation, Johnston watches as the waves crash onto the shore through the office windows. "Because I'll have to tell her that I fathered another child with this woman. Abigail has a half-brother, and she'll never forgive that. Teena discovered this the night before her death," he confesses.

This seems to be the zenith of today's discussion and now is a time for reflection. Johnston agrees because he has no idea what to do. He has just unburdened himself of the deepest, darkest secret of his life and now wants to retreat to his own private corner of the world as if time will make it all go away.

"I'm not ready to share any of this with my daughter," Johnston declares. "I haven't been able to tell her about David for seven years. Why would I now? How will that repair the damage I've done at this point in time? And it's not just Abigail I have to consider; her brother will have to know as well. He's off at college, starting his own life.

How on earth will he ever forgive me? Abigail will leave soon and then the dust can settle until a better time to introduce them all."

There is silence in the office for some time before Johnston makes his decision, "I'm not prepared to tell Abigail any of this so there is no need for me to stay for her appointment. I'm sorry, Taylor, I just can't do this yet."

"There is no need for apologies, Johnston. I understand what a shock this news would be to your children. I also believe that Abigail senses the secret, though she believes it's about Teena and not your other family. At some point, you will need to lay all of this out on the table, and I promise waiting longer will not make the conversation easier." I watch Johnston as he thinks about what I've said. "I'd also recommend breaking the news in the presence of a professional to help navigate the emotions that will surely erupt. Would you consider this option?" I ask.

"Yes. That's probably the best way to present or confess my secret. This news affects so many people in my life and it's that expense that scares me most. Will I lose some of them? I could potentially lose all of them to this secret and the timing, and that I would never recover from." Johnston remains stoic in the chair, but his face becomes flush.

"I am available for your family anytime; I hope you know that. If you'd prefer someone else to be present, I can make a very good recommendation. Whatever you decide, please let me help. You're not in this alone."

The conversation wanes as Johnston shuts down and withdraws from talking any longer, so I end the session. "I will let Abigail know that you did meet with me but are not ready to share all of the details of your marriage with Teena. She will respect that, I think."

After Johnston leaves, a sudden feeling of confusion comes over me and I can't clear my mind of the dozen thoughts circling in my brain. Have I simply uncovered too many secrets for my professional and personal psyche to process at once? There are Calvin's secrets, Johnston's secret, and the one that naturally affected me the most,

Jake's many secrets. Through the overwhelming fog, one thing becomes crystal clear. I need to get away for a long weekend.

A sense of guilt washes over. *Who is running away now?* I'm not running from anything; I need to escape to a neutral place where I can think straight and clear my mind. Someplace no one knows me, and I know no one else. I'll sit on the sand up north and let the ocean air clear the noise from my brain, then I can return to be my best for my clients, my friend, and most of all, myself.

 Reflections

After a week of planning, I am heading up PCH toward one of my favorite spots along the ocean. It is a high spot and a promontory that offers a panoramic view of the Pacific. It isn't the twisted, lone eucalyptus scene of the California central coast that inspires so many calendar makers, but it is close. As I pull up, I try to remember the last time I was here with the Pacific stretched away to the horizon. The sea is rough today with white caps crashing onto the shore with heaving swells further out. Seagull's circle, squawk, and complain in their endless search for food. The scene has an immediate suggestion that the world is still here and moving on. The breaks prove it as they come to shore in a steady shush in bubbling, white, frothy foam. Someone once mentioned that the surf was eternal; interesting and poetic when you think about it. The tide will come in and go out. Forever.

Yes, it had been a long time since my last visit. Has my life been so "together" since then that I didn't feel I needed this solitude for reflection? It seems doubtful. When I think about my life, as long as I can remember, my focus has been on other people's issues and none I couldn't handle. But not now. Now I have a problem, one that has threatened my very essence and the image I have of myself as a balanced, focused, and successful woman living the life I always wanted. I am here to adjust my vision going forward.

I find myself wondering if I am ready to walk away from my marriage. Jake committed the apex of sins by having affairs, multiple affairs, during our entire time together. I may have reacted quickly with my decision to end things with him. I've been considering the advice I'd give my clients—take contemplative time to think through your options before taking action. Was I hasty in declaring the marriage over to Jake? I have made this short journey to be thoughtful and consider what I want and what I don't.

After checking into a beach view room in the small hotel near Pismo Beach, I head to the beach for the rest of the afternoon. Toes in the sand, and my head clearing with each wave that recedes from shore.

My favorite beach spot will help to reset my compass and set me on the path to an honest future without lies and betrayal. If my choice is to end things by the end of the weekend, I can make this change with the support of Annette, though she is deep into her own major life event with Calvin's return. Brett is proving to be more than just a mentor. He is stepping up as a friend, one I didn't realize has been there for me all this time.

Once settled on the sand, my eyes become heavy, and my mind wanders to the past, those early days with Jake when I was innocent and in love. Our relationship was easy and carefree. How was Jake able to hide so much of himself from me? It's clear that he was one person with me and a different person when away. Does he fit the definition of a psychopath or just antisocial personality disorder? Does he have a sex addiction?

As my brain spirals down the psycho definitions and possible diagnoses, my eyes suddenly pop open. *Is someone else here?* My heart is pounding in my chest and my stomach tightens. Again, there is no one else around; I am alone on the beach. This feeling of being watched has crept up on me too many times in recent months. Why? What is the cause of this? I am officially taunted so I gather my things and head to my room.

As I pass shrubs and reeds along the dunes, I hold my breath that no one appears suddenly and gives me a heart attack. I find my pace becoming quicker the closer I get to the hotel grounds. Perspiration puddles on my face and runs down my back. But I can't stop until I'm in my room and locked. Once inside, I have the need to talk to someone, so I pull out my cell and make a call.

Two hours later, Brett meets me at the hotel restaurant. I was too shaken up to leave the comfort of these walls, so I chose the closest restaurant available. He looks concerned and frankly, it feels nice to have someone concerned about me. How selfish is that? It's a foreign feeling but I want to relish it for now.

Drinks are ordered and although I'm not much of a drinker, I'm going to indulge and slip into a mellower state of mind and enjoy Brett's company and forget the turmoil of my life.

He says, "I've never seen you looked so . . .so. . ."

"Casual?"

"Yeah. That's the right adjective."

"I am feeling calmer and relaxed. I see what happens living with blinders on can do to one's life. The fact that I completely missed any cues of Jake's infidelities during our entire marriage is a wakeup call. I've accepted that I'll never trust him like I want to be able to trust a partner, so barring a miracle, I'm moving forward on my own."

"Did you talk to Roz about your decision? Does Jake know where your head is at?"

The drinks arrive and I take a big sip of mine. Brett is still gazing my way. "Yes, and not exactly."

"How so?"

"Well, I told Roz my trust couldn't be repaired with time and no amount of couples therapy will change that. Jake is in denial and keeps calling asking to meet and talk about a possible reconciliation."

His eyes are focused deeply into mine and says, "Ouch. Not uncommon though."

"Yeah. Frankly, originally, I thought I'd do anything to work things out until he confessed to multiple affairs throughout the twelve years we were together. This has been a profound experience. When I think of my professional recommendations I've given to clients after one confesses infidelity, I'm appalled. I tell them to *reassess your lives with an open mind and if it is still basically good and you still love each other, begin the process of healing.* I can see the words rolling out of my mouth. *One step at a time. Start with romantic dates. Don't rush into sex as if the physical act alone will mend your broken heart. Take it slow I'd caution.* But now. . ."

"Now?"

I can't get the words out, but Brett, the ever-patient therapist, waits.

I blurt out, "Life is just too short for dishonesty. We deserve the best for ourselves and if that means working through this kind of crap for some couples, then more power to them. For others, the destruction of trust and faith is irreparable, and I shouldn't feel guilty for wanting more from a partner. For saying enough."

Brett reaches over and takes my hands as tears well in my eyes.

"But, how in hell do I begin to forget? How long until the healing begins? God knows who these other women are that Jake has been with? I sure look the fool, don't I? The worst part of this is what I do for a living! I excavate the buried issues of other people's problems; help clients identify them and resolve them. I never saw this coming."

Brett says, "I hear that you're embarrassed about this. You think you should have seen it coming. But, Taylor, you're looking at it as a professional. None of us in this field examine our own lives like we do our clients lives. It's not so much, I don't think, that we're so involved in our practice but more that we practice what we preach: trust, faith, and maybe contentedness."

Brett is a sweet man and is trying to help me. But now, subconsciously maybe, I am wondering about him. *He is certainly an attractive man. Why no wife? Why no girlfriend?*

Then I chastise myself. *Why would I doubt Brett?* His kiss was so sweet. So sweet in fact I can't forget it. But is this the time to engage in a new relationship? How can I begin something when I haven't even brought my marriage to an end? I don't understand myself right now. How can I bring another person into my situation? Then why did I call him?

Brett asks, "Taylor, don't go trying to figure out life in one fell swoop. We know that life is a complicated thing. Maybe we wish that it wasn't or that it's an exaggeration to make us feel needed as therapists, but it is complex. We deal with every human emotion in every type of person and we both know that no two lives are alike."

If nothing else, Brett has me thinking. I can't disagree with anything he's said. I can't question his professionalism, nor, as far as I know, his morals. Yet, let's face it, I've only dealt with him on a professional level. Other than him being a supportive colleague, I can't vouch for his morals. Not really.

I take a sip and look over the top of my martini glass at him. Could the inkling of romance be coloring my judgment?

Brett breaks the prevailing silence, "Do you ever wonder about the success rate in your practice? How many people we really help? I mean that we're sure of. I know that sometimes it looks like we've been successful but let's face it, when you consider medicine as a whole, psychology is still the poor boy."

I have an answer for him. "I see my practice as identifying the feelings and behaviors that are in play. I know that often the trick is to get the patient to be honest about what emotion we are dealing with; and pride and shame often veils the real problem underneath."

"So true." He smiles now. The smile gets me curious, "What?"

"Whenever I begin to take myself too seriously in this business and believe that I'm being effective, I'm reminded of a comedian. When someone asks the shrink, 'How many patients do you have?' The shrink says, 'About fifty.' Then he's asked, 'How many have you cured?' He thinks a minute and says, 'None, but we're making good progress.'"

"Is that how you open your conference presentations?" Now, I have a question for Brett that pertains to both our professional and my personal lives. "In your opinion, what is the most difficult emotion that therapists face?"

"No doubt about it, love. For me, love is universal and afflicts both genders. It is certainly a strong emotion, I would venture to say one of the most powerful, but still the most misunderstood."

"Do you have a definition of love that you find practicable? I mean one that you use in your work. And," I add, knowing I am being bold, "in your personal life?"

"Like most humans, I can only describe it from my personal perspective. I know what we think it means but then most of us are confused by it. It comes to us at a young age, and for many, in adulthood, it is often cloaked in a less noble emotion, lust. Animals too seem to manifest love but in a vastly different way than we mere humans. They love and protect their young, yet the mating impulse is not connected to love like us humans—that is, being bound to one another. And as much as the animals love their young, they're practical. Once they have taught them to fend for themselves and survive, they are abandoned. I've never forgotten a naturalist's documentary that follows the she bear abandoning her cubs at the beginning of or about their third birthday; the cubs just stand for a moment, perplexed, then run after her, but she just shucks them. And that's it. They are on their own to perpetuate their life cycle and she's off to mate again and birth more cubs."

The story almost makes me cry. Or maybe it is just the mood I'm in and the alcohol is making me feel sappy. "I agree about love. There is nothing more perplexing for humans."

Brett's gaze is still deep in mine. I can't look away or ignore them even if I want to, which I don't. He says, "The best way I can define love comes from the bible. Many people won't accept that because their ideal of love has nothing to do with religion or the 'love' of God."

"So," I say, "your definition has nothing to do with God or divinity?"

"No, not really, yet it comes from the bible."

"What part?"

He looks at me, "Corinthians."

I cock my head and gaze at him. "The one used in weddings?"

"Yes. The one that says, 'Love is patient but not envious or boastful or arrogant or rude. It does not insist on its own way. It is not irritable or resentful. It does not rejoice in wrongdoing but rejoices in the truth. It bears all things, believes all things, hopes all things, and endures all things. Prophecies, they will come to an end, as knowledge will come to an end. Of faith, hope and love, love is the greatest. Love will never end.'" He pauses.

"I know it seems surreal and above man's abilities, considering the imperfection of man. But it is the one that resonates with me. If I had a love with only one of those qualities, I would consider myself lucky in life."

Brett has spoken a mouthful and I am a bit awed. Here is a man of ideals. That is if he is honest, and I have no reason to think he isn't. I am being as generous as I can, considering my present distrust of men based on my personal situation.

Brett asks, "Do you honestly feel that you and Jake cannot work this out?"

"I was hopeful when I only knew about the affair with Linda. Now. . .there is no way. Knowing that he's been screwing around all these years makes it impossible for me forgive him. I wouldn't know where to start." I say ending in an audible sigh.

He gazes at me then asks, "Do you believe love never ends, that we love even beyond the grave?"

"I'd like to think so."

"But it's too difficult?"

"Yeah, at least at this point in my life," I reply.

"What are you going to do?"

I stare into his green eyes. What the heck was I looking for? Some magical insight? To what questions?"

It is early evening, and we are the only ones left from the lunch crowd, so we discuss leaving. He walks me to my car, and as I get in, I lower my sunglasses and wonder what to say when Brett says, "Promise me you'll keep me up to date."

All I can do is give him a tepid smile and promise I will. He leans down and gives me a kiss on the cheek, which feels nice. And kind. And loving?

On the way back southward the next morning, I feel good about my decision about my marriage; I deserve better than a man who cannot be committed to me wholly. I'll be fine with the support of friends and my work.

I collect Cali from the boarders and head home. There is nothing like a dog's company. They love without motive or self-interest. They love without inhibition. They love without abandon. They love unconditionally.

I fix myself a quick meal then stand in the middle of the living room taking in the quiet and solitude that is my new life when the phone rings, breaking my melancholy, thoughtful mood. The caller ID shows Jake's number, so I answer.

His voice, in the preliminary *hi, how are you* is soft and mellow. It doesn't sound like him. Not to say he was never mellow, but tonight, he sounds rather pathetic. The slight slur tells me he has been drinking. "Did you get anything from the meeting with Roz the other day?"

A long, awkward silence fills the space between us, and I don't want to discuss getting a divorce over the phone, so I say, "Jake, you don't sound like you're in the right frame of mind for this conversation. You sound more like you need a friend to talk to. That isn't me."

"Taylor, no. Let me explain." Then the phone line becomes awkwardly silent.

"Again, Jake, it's not the right time. Think things over when you don't have a drink in your hand and we'll meet to talk."

After twelve years of thinking everything was fine only to learn otherwise, I wasn't feeling particularly empathetic toward him now. A dozen years of cheating with as many women left me feeling hurt and angry but resolute in my decision to move on without him. I'd lost my melancholy mood and went to bed muttering, *Men, can any of them be trusted?*

MONTEREY

I feel somewhat better in the morning. Memories of Brett and his touching and caring ways warms my injured heart.

I've blocked off time first thing to spend with Annette at The Perk. As she stirs sugar into her cup, she asks, "What's your impression of Calvin's story?"

I gaze at her. "Are you suggesting that there is something about his story you question?" Even as she speaks, I realize that, *hey this is the new Taylor. Do I still believe everything I hear?*

"I don't know, Taylor, some parts of it, you have to admit, are bizarre. Don't you think the timing of Calvin's disappearance and Wes appearing is coincidental? And then Wes disappearing when Calvin turns up again after five years?"

"Yeah, I thought the same thing. But is there a reason to believe that there is something fishy about it? I mean, why would they come and go from your life, from the business? What could be gained?"

"Frankly, I haven't a clue, but this is all so surreal."

"Well, let's take one thing at a time," I say in my professional and calm way.

"Yeah, what do you think is next?"

"You and Calvin are working through the reconciliation, but the business has a huge impact on your livelihood as well. Perhaps a meeting with you, Calvin, Gabriel, and Wes to decide on equities and so forth. Getting that aspect of your lives outlined may help Calvin make a plan and, that will help you both. Besides, changes may be in order."

Annette curls her upper lip. "What more changes could possibly be in order? I've had my fill of changes for the next decade, thank you. That's fair, isn't it?"

"Annette, if it were up to me, you wouldn't experience another change unless you initiated it! You've been a champ the past several years and counting; losing your husband, reinventing yourself, then your husband returning out of the blue. I admire your strength and tenacity, girl!"

Annette takes my hand and pats it. "You're my rock, Taylor. I don't know what I'd do without you."

I really didn't feel like Annette's rock or anybody else's. I was at the lowest point in my life and questioning everything. I hope the feeling doesn't last long and I can move past the betrayal by my husband of twelve years who has been cheating on me and I never hurt so much in my life.

When I think about seeking solace in Brett's arms, I feel something deep down within me. It's a warning saying, *don't go looking for the perfect love. Don't go looking for perfection on the rebound. You're bound to be disappointed.* What would hurt even more would be, on the rebound, if I threw myself into Brett's arms, and he, God forbid, turned out to be a disappointment, my despair would be bottomless. No, I don't want to go there. At least, not now when I'm feeling overly vulnerable. I need to protect my ego fearlessly, like a mother bear guards her cub.

Annette and I part, each going in different directions. She is meeting up with Calvin and I am returning to my dog at home.

Back home, I am alone, and finding it feeling less of a sanctuary right now. The walls feel more like a prison, and I don't feel like working. I reconsider a longer escape up the coast and ask my service to call my clients and reschedule the remainder of the week's appointments so I can run away and readjust my attitude.

I know it will be helpful, and I'd never be against such a recommendation for my clients as the popular image of getaways is self-introspection and relaxation. This sounded good, so I, with much guilt, again drop Cali off at the kennel, pack a bag, and set out up the coast.

The ocean is in my plans, but I also want to avoid places Jake and I had stayed. Four hours later, I am at a cliff side resort on the Monterey Peninsula. One of the reasons for selecting it is its natural beauty, but also because I am tired of driving. I've always found driving alone quite tedious. I am a social animal and need people; I need conversation. But not today or tomorrow. This week is about re-balancing my head and heart through the rhythm of the waves.

Peninsula Pines

Peninsula Pines is a beautiful hotel in a rustic setting. The endless vistas of the Pacific and the rolling surf are breathtaking. The blue waters below the cliffs sparkle in the afternoon sun with the brilliance of a million diamonds.

The room décor is pastoral with a lot of pictures and sketches of birds and wildlife and a curious fox overlooks my bed.

My plan is to immediately explore the area after unpacking but first, I lose my shoes and stretch out on the bed. The next thing I know, long shadows are creeping across my room and it is dinnertime.

I can't remember the last time I sat down to dinner alone in a restaurant; I find it more discomforting than I considered. Nobody else was alone, just couples and a few kids. I order a martini to help ease me into this new bachelorette mindset. I had changed for dinner and now I'm reassessing my chosen dinner attire. Is my skirt too long? Is my top too conservative? I am immediately self-conscious, and for no real reason. Maybe it is paranoia but did the waiter give me a double take? Did he wonder why I was alone or was he gauging his chances with a single woman staying at the hotel?

I make a concerted effort to keep my eyes forward noticing what is going on around me with my peripherals only. It seems to take forever for my dinner to arrive so I can at least appear busy eating it. I'm glad I brought a book along to pass the time.

After a dinner of fresh salmon and asparagus, I find the sun is still lingering on the horizon, so I make my way to a nearby gazebo on the cliff's edge only to find it occupied by a starry-eyed young couple probably on their honeymoon. In as smooth a manner as I can manage, I change course until I find myself mesmerized by the huge basketball of an orb begin to settle behind the choppy waters.

Once it is dark, I head back to my oceanside room while continuing to avert my eyes from others and manage only a cursory nod to those I cannot avoid.

In the haven of my room, I plop myself down on the bed and resist the temptation to turn on the TV for mere distraction. In my analytical way, I know that I need to think about why I am here and how to move ahead without Jake in my life. After hearing about Jake's other women, I quickly came to understand that I am less interested in his needs and problems, and that I need to focus on me and my future now. Jake certainly could have not confessed to multiple affairs, and rather than look at it as a courageous and positive thing, I felt just the opposite. I now see him as a compulsive philanderer. Since we never went through any rough patches in our twelve years' together, I am perplexed by his need for other women. Did I fail him in the bedroom? Was I too boring? Too conventional? Was I not there for him emotionally? This would normally be my innate line of thinking, but I find it is not. I am damn hurt, and I don't care why he did it. Maybe this path of thinking is immature and unsensible, but I'm not a saint either. I just can't conceive of forgiving him, but might time change my resoluteness?

Eventually, after an hour of making a list of pros and cons, I surrender and watch TV until finally, sleep comes.

In the morning, I am awakened by the chirping of my cell phone next to me on the nightstand. Groggily, I answer. It is Brett. His voice is full of concern. "Taylor. I was worried. Your service said you were unavailable all week."

"No need for concern, Brett. I'm just taking some much-needed time off."

"Oh, sure," he said, sounding relieved. "Okay, I won't bother you again. You have my number if you need me. Right?"

"Of course. And thanks for calling."

I don't feel thankful, but it was the polite thing to say. Not that I was rude, but I probably was a bit short. Brett is, after all, a naturally caring person. I promise myself to make it up to him when I get home.

Now awake, I prepare to start my day with breakfast then a long hike followed by beach time. A trek along the cliffs aside the beautiful Pacific is calling for me.

The surf is smashing against the shoreline rocks and shooting skyward in a dramatic display. Some of the water swirls and gushes around the rocks creating interesting eddies and channels of foamy, white bubbly water. There are already people planting themselves on the beach.

I'm not any more comfortable at breakfast than at dinner, but the wonderful food took my mind off of feeling self-conscious. Afterward, I pick up a brochure at the front desk describing a walking trail that begins on the property and winds its way up the coast. This is for me. I buy trail mix at the hotel shop, stuff it and a banana from breakfast in my jacket pocket, and set out.

The trail follows the coast and is lined with conifers, California pine, and the occasional eucalyptus.

I can only marvel at the natural beauty and when I meet fellow hikers on the trail, I give them a nod.

A couple of hours into the hike, I feel tired enough to perch on a rock with a good view of the ocean. I have worked up an appetite, so I munch on some trail mix and contemplate what brought me here—to think about my future, with or without my husband.

I do this for a living, dissect people's problems. Now, I'm struggling how to handle my own crisis. I already felt that Jake and I were through. How on earth could I go on knowing what I do? Yet wasn't a strong love supposed to be able to confront and overcome anything? What had Brett said, "Love is never resentful. Love bears all things, believes all things, hopes all things . . . and what was the most important? Ah yes, endures all things."

Am I capable of all that? At first glance, it doesn't seem so. I am hurt. And I *am* resentful. I ponder if I can bear all things. *Hoping* all things. And finally, *enduring* all things.

This gets me thinking about the Bible. Is it possible in real life situations to follow the Bible's teachings and commandments? Isn't that its purpose? To guide us and heck, to live by? So, when it comes to real life, am I doubting the words of the apostles and God himself?

After more soul searching, I conclude that I am not the person I think I am. I am hurt and that's all I've focused on. The things in the Bible seem to be for people with a lot more religious conviction and strength than I have right now.

I am deep into these thoughts when a man stops at my rock. He eyes it and looks like he is going to sit near me. I don't want to act like a hysterical female so at first, I do nothing. I hardly acknowledge him but when he speaks, I must respond to him.

He is about my age, slim and good-looking enough. He's wearing a pair of tan hiking shorts and a sweater draped over his shoulders that was in style a decade earlier. He says, "Did you set out from the hotel?"

I nod.

"I thought I recognized you from dinner last night. I guess this is the spot when you're tired enough to stop. Do you hike much?"

I reply, "No, not really," thinking this left him no room to go with the conversation but that doesn't deter him.

"How do you like the hotel?"

"I've only been here a day, but it's very nice," I say.

"How long are you staying?" the stranger asks.

I hesitate. Was this an inquisition? "I . . . I don't know exactly. Just a couple of days."

He nods, but I think that I've already given him more information than I want. When was the last time I talked with a man who wasn't in some sort of social setting, like a party or something? Before I can recall, he asks, "Am I bothering you? I have a motor mouth I'm afraid, and not used to solitude."

This gives me an opening to ask him some obvious questions, but I don't. I'm just not that interested in the stranger who is sharing this boulder. Instead, I think the silence will give him a hint that I'm not in the mood for company. It doesn't.

"I'm on my way up to Oregon and when I saw this spot, I had to get off the road early to indulge myself." The stranger continued.

"I can see that." Hesitantly, I queried, "What's in Oregon?"

"Oh, I'm on my way to a medical convention. I could have taken a plane, but I thought, *when am I going to have a chance to see the California coast up close?*"

"It's a beautiful place," was all I could muster.

Thankfully, he seemed to have said enough and we both kept our gaze on the ocean and the circling sea gulls, then in the distance, a fully rigged schooner appeared on the horizon.

The man broke the silence, "I think that's one of those vacation schooners they advertise. You know the sailing trips? The ones they call 'barefoot adventures?'"

"Yes, I suppose so. It seems I always had an interest in doing it but never have."

"Yeah, life gets busy; you only get to do a tiny percentage of what you'd like to."

Finally, I realize this man means no harm to me and the conversation reaches a comfortable level and for the next half hour, we chat about all kinds of things avoiding topics too personal in nature.

When I get up to head back to the hotel, he rises too but heads in the opposite direction. "See you around the hotel," he says as we part ways.

"Sure," I say.

Well, that wasn't too bad, my first conversation with a man who wasn't trying to help me or reconcile with me. Just two people talking about nothing in particular.

When I get back to the hotel, it was too late for lunch, but the trail mix and the banana had sustained me and leaves me wondering what to do next. There is a pool as well as the beach below the cliffs. I opt for the beach. So, I quick change into my swimsuit, a black one piece, grab a beach blanket and sunscreen, then make my way down the wooden steps to the beach. It is mid-afternoon and empty now which suits me fine.

After getting comfortable on the warm afternoon sand, my hope is to forget everything for a while. The surf swooshes in, the seagulls squawk, and then a dark shadow covers me. Startled, I look up and am relieved to see it isn't the man going to Oregon, just a hotel waiter asking me if I'd like a drink, and soon, I have a Cosmopolitan in hand. The waiter and I exchanged pleasantries. He lingered a little longer than one would expect but was soon on his way.

What did I expect? I may be projecting a particular image. Maybe a little enigmatic right now, stirring a bit of curiosity in others. But that would fade fast if they learned I was just another cheated-on wife, trying to figure out life's plan.

A couple of hours lapse, then I return to my room, but I am beginning to feel isolated and lonely, so I found a clear station on the radio. As I listen carefully to the words of the love songs, something I never really had done before, I hear the lyrics speak of heartbreak, and loneliness, and pain. Many country songs leaned into revenge and action by the brokenhearted.

My thoughts drift back to the stranger on the hiking trail. He was pleasant enough, a bit chatty for never having had an encounter before, but maybe it was nerves. I never did catch his name.

I had some trepidation about going to dinner that night but refused to let it beat me into ordering room service. I'd put on a comfortable dress and go.

The hiker was there, and he too was alone. I cringed and hoped he wouldn't come over to my table. I hated the imagery of the lonely single woman being hit on. But he didn't make any advances. However, after dinner, he caught me in the lobby, "I couldn't help but notice you're alone too. Can I interest you in a night cap? We can have it on the patio."

It felt easier to accept than not, so I agreed. Soon, we were seated above the sea, watching the sun sinking ever so slowly. "Ever been to the tropics?" he asked.

"Yes, Cabo and Acapulco."

"So, you know about the green line when the sun goes down."

I look blankly at him.

He says, "Just before the sun finally clears the horizon, a green line of light shoots out. Something to do with atmospherics."

"Interesting," I reply. "I'd never heard about that phenomenon."

He grins. "No, it isn't that interesting, just a bumbler's way of making conversation."

We both laugh and the conversation goes more smoothly from there. Much like the afternoon, we just talk about anything that comes to mind.

At the end of the evening, we make our excuses and head back to our respective rooms.

Early the next morning, as I am again setting out for the trail, I come across him packing up the trunk of a Volvo. I ask, "Off to Oregon?"

He turns. "Oh, hi. Yeah, enough lingering. Who am I kidding? I'm a busy man who tried to be footloose for a day. Yeah, I gotta go."

We stand silently as he fishes a business card out of his pocket and says, "You're a great listener. If you ever want someone to talk to, please give me a call."

Imprinted on the card is "Dr. Walter Slezak, Pediatrician." I reply, "Thanks, maybe I will."

He extends his hand for a shake, gets in his car, and with an over-the-shoulder smile, is gone.

Now, who is the enigmatic one? Is he single? Divorced? Just lonely? Troubled? What? As I hit the trail, I had to think. This is probably how it starts, a casual meeting, an easiness with one another. But at our age, each person is probably toting a lot of emotional baggage. I imagine what a relationship might be with this man I barely know before the trail and surroundings capture my attention.

When I stop and rest on the same rock as the previous day, Brett fills my thoughts. Could I possibly consider an intimate relationship with him? I've known him for so long yet seem to know so little about him, his personal life. What difference did that make? Perhaps, it was time to delve into a deeper connection with him now that I plan to be single again.

I spend most of my day on the beach, sunbathing and gazing out to sea. In the morning, I'll be heading back south to Chelsea. My decision is made.

Pacific Crest

Jake is eager to get on with couples counseling with Roz, but my decision is made. I want to continue counseling on my own and file for divorce when my feelings are less raw.

The sessions re-affirm what I already knew and, in fact, had counseled clients many times myself. If the couple still loved each other, it was possible to get over the pain of betrayal. My hang up is it wasn't just one betrayal but many. And, if I had no idea he was unhappy in the past, how would I know in the future? That he was unfulfilled again because it seems the problem is that Jake isn't getting what he needs from our relationship. I had no idea what I could do to change that, especially when I never had a clue about it in the first place.

Jake's truth-dumping revealed that the women involved in his escapades were not necessarily better looking or younger than me nor provided a better lifestyle. Unfortunately, I can't be sure he's been telling the truth. I can see him not wanting to hurt me and say these things about the other women. Maybe on a superficial level, I could see someone younger, someone prettier, or sexier. But that wasn't necessarily our situation, so no amount of health clubs and Victoria Secret lingerie was going to keep him happy at home. At least in my mind.

I devote my attention to my practice and for a while, that was enough to keep my mind off these marital problems. My regulars keep me on my toes and working with Annette and Calvin is a satisfactory work in progress. The two are devoted to working through the pains of the previous five years and Calvin is doing what he needs to answer all her questions and get his memory back.

Working with these two is not business-as-usual for me. By that, I mean sitting in my office and rehashing old disagreements and arguments, nor does picking apart each detail of Calvin's experience in Oregon, so I suggest we drive to the Pacific Crest surf shop. My thinking is that it may spark a memory or clear a path for Calvin and Gabriel to discuss where he fits in the new structure even with Wes in the wind.

Upon my arrival at Pacific Crest, Annette and Calvin are waiting for me out front of the building with Gabriel just looking at the exterior with large hand gestures, smiles, nods, and laughter.

Annette makes a beeline for me and gives a hug. "Have you ever been here?" she asks.

"I have not. It's much larger than I was imagining." I reply as we walk to the two men still locked in conversation.

"Hi Gabriel. Calvin." I give Calvin a hug and shake Gabriel's hand, then we all enter the single-story building. The exterior is nothing fancy at all; concrete walls with substantial metal beams anchoring each corner. They have a heavy patina-rust color that adds life to the gray.

We walk into the reception area that is roomy and stark with surfboards mounted on the walls, a desk to the back of the room, one large round table, and concrete floors stained in hues of blue making it feel like walking on water. After a tour of the shop where, as Gabriel says, the magic happens and construction brings the surfboards to life, we all gather around the table in the front room.

Gabriel brings a six pack of beer and continues enthusiastically telling Calvin about the new logo and improvements to the boards he's been customizing for their clientele.

"Just like you thought, using the newer polyurethane altered the weight for better buoyancy and performance on the water." Gabriel was smiling and gesturing as he talked about beginner boards on up to professional and the who's who list of new customers.

Calvin interrupts, "Wow, I've missed so much, and it sounds like there's been a lot of exciting times here. Sorry I missed them."

"You're back now, dude." Gabriel reassures his friend. "Just wait until you see some of the names of our customers. Man, they include the top five surfers in the world!"

Calvin nearly falls off the chair, "Holy shit! For real?"

"No kiddin', dude." Gabriel says shaking his head from side to side.

As they continue their conversation, my eyes wander around the room to a spot filled with about a dozen photos meticulously organized on the wall behind the lone desk. I casually walk there with Annette who explains it is her wall of memories—pictures taken before Calvin's disappearance—the opening of the shop, when Gabriel joined, the guys with customers at the beach during competitions, and one with three men: Calvin, Gabriel, and another I am surprised to recognize.

"Who is this with the guys?" I ask Annette.

"That's Wes."

My jaw becomes slack, lip's part, but nothing comes out. My mouth suddenly can't make a sound.

"What is it?" Annette asks.

Mouth slightly open, head rolling left the right. "That's the man."

Annette's brows furrow, "What man? What are you trying to say?"

"That's the man. You know, the one who approached me at Peninsula Pines. He said his name was Walter Slezak and that he was a pediatrician. What the hell? This can't be a coincidence. You think?"

Annette looks confused. "Maybe they just look similar. I mean, what are the odds of it really being Wes? And you never met before."

"I'm telling you; this is the same guy. I swear to you."

From behind us, "What is it?" Calvin asks.

"Taylor says that Wes is actually the guy that approached her on the hike at Peninsula Pines. Strange, right?"

On cue, both men turn toward me in unison.

"Are you sure?" Calvin asks as Gabriel says, "It just can't be. At least I don't see how it could be. You think it is?"

"Guys, it's the same man. Either his name is Wes or it's Walter. Maybe it's neither and he's a total scammer, but this is the same guy on the hike."

The room falls quiet for several minutes as all let the revelation settle in. The fact that Gabriel wasn't totally comfortable with him, the bar fight in Oregon, the man on the hike telling me he's from Oregon all amounts to too much coincidence.

"I have to tell you now that I've felt like someone has been watching me at times. I know by the little hairs standing erect on my neck and chills sliding down my spine. It's been going on for a couple of weeks."

"That's around the same time C.J. got back and Wes went AWOL," Gabriel shares.

"Why would he be following me? I don't think we ever met before my stay at Peninsula Pines. I don't understand it; I can't connect the dots here. I have no history with Wes. How would he even know who I am?" By now, I'm pacing the concrete floor and the others are silent.

"Listen, you all stay here and talk about Calvin's return to Pacific Crest. I'm heading back to my office. Annette, I'll call you later . . . and don't worry about—" I whisper in my friends' ear as we hug goodbye.

Once inside my Prius, I lock the doors. This is the first time I can recall ever doing this before starting my car. Am I target now?

DATE NIGHT

After months of staving off Brett's invitations to dinner or movies, I finally give in. We made plans before the visit to Pacific Crest and the realization that the man I inadvertently met at Peninsula Pines was indeed Wes, the missing partner of Gabriel. I had considered canceling the date, but then convinced myself that I deserved a day out to forget about everything happening and just enjoy socializing with Brett for a change.

When Brett arrives on Saturday morning, he looks like he has taken special care to dress nicely, though much more casually than the sport jacket during the week. The day was lovely and perfect for a ride in his convertible. Conversation was easy and we laughed carefreely like never before.

The restaurant he picked is romantic and makes me wonder for the first time, how far am I willing to take this? Brett is a sweetheart, an old friend, but now he is developing into a new persona, that of a suitor and though I am still feeling hesitance, I am ready to let go of the past.

"How was your, uh, vacation a few weeks back?"

I smile. "I didn't plan it as a vacation, but more as therapy."

"Okay, how did the therapy go?"

I lapse thoughtfully. *How did it go?* I gaze at him. "I don't know how to answer you."

He cocks his head. "What do you mean?"

I hesitate. "I don't know whether to answer you as a friend, as a colleague, or as someone who I want to get closer to."

"Which would you prefer?"

I had to grin. "We sound like teenagers."

He returns the grin. "I know what you mean. I was thinking the same thing." Then adds, "Well, we're old friends so we don't have to go through the whole routine of learning about one another through a series of dates. Although I can't think of anything I'd like better than more dates."

I smile. He says, "So you can see, I've thrown away my therapist hat. I'm just Brett, a man who cares about you. I'd like to find out how I go about learning more about you."

"You mean as a friend, colleague, or lover?"

"Exactly," he quips.

"I know one thing. I'm not going to answer that with a question. Just treat me like you would any other date."

We sip our drinks and give the waitress our orders. That took us away from the conversation for a few minutes. When we are back looking into one another's eyes, I say, "It occurs to me, you never talk about your love life or who you are dating."

"That's true. Well, let me fill you in. I'm real busy and have neglected my social life to a great degree. But there is a lady across town who fixes me breakfast occasionally."

I gaze at him. How odd. You know someone for years and never picture him eating breakfast with someone.

He saw something in my demeanor as I think this over. "What are you doing?" he asks, "Picturing me in bed with someone?"

I'm beginning to feel the alcohol kick in and I almost giggle. "Yes, I am."

"And?"

More nervous laughter. Am I being a silly, schoolgirl? I look at him and say, "I never knew you had such big muscles."

We both break into laughter, and it feels wonderful . . . freeing. It feels good to be carefree which is allowing me to forget my worries and my lack of a . . . a what? Lust for life? Yeah, that was it or at least close to it. I purposely avoid sharing the recent revelation of the man's identity on the hike as being Wes—the long-lost business partner of Gabriel at Pacific Crest. Instead, we have a great time. I engage in the conversation and indulge in another martini. Brett, ever practical, limits himself to two, and I think that is mostly so that I am not drinking alone.

For the next couple of hours, we share details of our childhoods that we didn't know. School events, boyfriends and girlfriends of simpler times, and parents that made parenting look easy. The evening ends with a kiss goodnight on my doorstep and me wanting more of Brett.

WES

Gabriel is on time as usual. He brings me a coffee and I graciously accept it as the hangover was still with me.

I sip gratefully. He says, "I've never seen you looking anything but a hundred percent together."

I look over the top of my coffee cup at him. "And now I don't?"

He grins. "You look a bit . . . uh . . ."

"Hung over?"

"Uh . . . Yes."

"Well, I am. Shrinks need an outlet too."

He sips his coffee. "I'm not judging."

"So," I continue, trying to regain control of the conversation, "how are things going at the shop now that Calvin is back?"

"Good. You know I thought it would be kinda awkward, but we're picking up where we left off."

"The business is doing well enough," I ask between sips, "to again include Calvin?"

"Oh yeah. One issue is with the new patent that was approved. Question is how do I compensate the long-lost Wes and determine C.J.'s worth cuz I don't know how much he contributed to the original idea. What is C.J.'s worth to the business now?"

"The surfboard patent." I stop. "Who came up with it?"

"Well, C.J. and I were working on it when he disappeared. But Wes was an aeronautical engineer at Boeing before he joined Pacific Crest. He designed things for airplanes. He could see the unique idea for a surfboard C.J. was pursuing and he applied the principles he used in designing wings for supersonic aircraft."

I reply, "Interesting."

"Yeah, other than that, things are going well for me. Is it awkward? You know, me talking about Wes when it turns out that he's the guy on the hike? That he lied about who he was and all?"

"No, not in this situation. I'm fine. Don't worry about me. I'm handling the realization on my end. All is good," I proclaim.

At the end of the session, I say, "Well, I'll see you next week. I hope everything continues to go well for you and Calvin."

"Thanks, Taylor, it's going to be easier said than done with Wes being MIA." And then he is gone.

Later that night after a play at the local theater, Brett and I stop at a coffee house for a snack. I must have drifted off because I was brought back to the moment by a kiss on the mouth.

"Sorry, it's business, nothing personal."

"So, I only get involved with one side of you. What's troubling you?" he asks.

"I was just thinking that I want to go up to Spencer, Oregon next weekend."

"Spencer? Isn't that where Annette's husband was found after years of being missing?"

"Same place."

I knew I couldn't keep him in the dark, "Yeah, I have a need to do some detective work up there. If only to tie up some loose ends."

"Like?" Brett was a man of few words. Brevity was his trademark.

"Between discovering that the stranger I met on the trail at Peninsula Pines was actually Wes, and things that Annette told me has raised some red flags and I need to check them out."

He waits for more, expecting me to share and be completely forthcoming with him.

"If Wes exposed himself to me while being MIA at the shop, then he's up to something. I don't know what, but it can't be good. Something in my gut says Wes was involved with Calvin's incident five years ago. I can't put my finger on it exactly, and I can't describe what I think I'll find, but I'll know it when I see it. And hopefully, this will reveal why I'm now Wes' object of obsession."

"You're planning to go alone?"

Meekly, I say, "Yes."

"I'm coming," he states bluntly.

I start to protest. "But. . ."

Brett shushes me, "But but but nothing. I'm coming. It sounds like it can be a rough town."

I smile. I must admit, it is nice to have someone worry about me, and I protest no more.

"Okay, I surrender, but before we go, could you do me a favor?" It's a rhetorical question because I had no doubt Brett would do it. "I know you used to do some evaluation work for Boeing, and you did it for a while. Do you still have any contacts at Boeing?"

"It depends, I guess. What do you need?"

"I'd like to get a more personal perspective on Wes Bradley. Like what people thought of him. What was his work record? And I guess, most importantly, why he left."

Brett considers the request a moment, "At first glance, one could conclude he left a gigantic industrial operation for the independence of his own business."

"My guess too, but they're only guesses at this point."

"Yeah, I still have some contacts. I'll try to find out more about him by the weekend."

SPENCER, OREGON

Saturday morning, we are on our way to Spencer, a small logging town just over the border in Oregon. It's another nice day, and the coastal highway was spectacular with its dramatic vistas on the ocean side and big woods effect on the other. But we had things to talk about and the scenery took second place.

Brett says, "The Human Resources people I dealt with put me onto Wes' immediate supervisor. Here's what the guy told me: Wes was a better-than-average designer, but he had an attitude."

My querulous glance at him from the passenger seat primes him. "Yeah, he didn't seem to be happy with the company's bonus program. He was a designer and so expected to earn more money than others for coming up with good designs that the company could use."

I say, "That could explain why he left and sought out private business."

"True. He worked at Boeing for three years, got along pretty well, but the bonus thing always seemed to bother him, and he left of his own accord five years ago."

"Just when Calvin disappeared."

"I guess that bolsters your theory, the one you told me where Calvin has some subconscious feelings about Wes."

"Right."

Brett asks, "What is it you hope to learn in Spencer?"

"Well, for one thing, I'm going to try to get a better handle on what Calvin was doing there and what happened to him beyond what the police and Annette know and what she's shared with me."

"Isn't that all in the police report?"

"Yeah, but it was a routine mugging outside a tough bar. They did no more than document it."

We arrive in Spencer by noon.

It was one of those towns that had once been prosperous, but the local logging operation was either played out or driven off by the Greenies. In any case, it was an old town as evidenced by the Victorian houses and the rundown condition of the streets.

We find a motel just north of town that seemed to be better than the ones we had passed driving into Spencer. This is new for me, and I didn't want to act the prude and demand separate rooms, so I settle on two beds.

Brett and I share reserved glances as we check out the room. He asks, "Do you know where you want to start?"

I respond, "Yes. At the bar where Calvin was mugged."

"Well, then I suggest we relax here for an hour or so, grab a bite at that diner down the road, then go to the bar."

I readily agree.

I don't know whether we were particularly tired from the drive or what, but we both laid on our respective beds and dozed off. I woke refreshed and ready for lunch.

The diner is one of those old railroad car units, fast fading from this country. It seems a better idea than fast food, so we settle into a window side booth.

The food isn't bad at all; I have a BLT and coffee, and Brett settles on a tuna sandwich.

We get into town late in the afternoon. "Do you think the bar will even be open this early?"

"If it's a working man's bar, and I suspect it is, it will be," Brett replies.

When we arrive at the bar, there are only motorcycles in the parking lot. I take a deep breath and walk beside Brett through the entrance. The bar isn't crowded and has the sleepy look of an old Western saloon on a weekday afternoon. We are dressed conservatively and look out of place amid the big bellies, beards, and tattoos.

We take our places at the far end of the bar, and shortly afterward, the thirty-fivish female bartender, worn out for her years, pauses lazily wiping glasses, and approaches us. We order drinks; ordinarily, I would have ordered a martini but that isn't on this bar's menu, so we have beer.

The bartender had only glanced at us when we came in but now gives us a more thorough going over. She has a tattoo on her neck which showed clearly with all the skin she exposed. It's a heart with an arrow through it, and another tattoo ran down her upper arm. Brett is trying to read it without being intrusive, but she catches his eye and mutters, "It says vampires aren't the only ones who suck." We both grin, but her once pretty face remains flat.

I pull Wes' picture from my bag and when she returns to us, I ask, "Excuse me, I'm doing some estate work for a client, and I wonder if you can tell me if you recognize this man."

She gives a cursory glance, and the answer was obvious. "No," she says.

This leaves us nothing else to do but go back to nursing our beers. When we finish, Brett pulls out a hundred-dollar bill to pay the tab and she gives it a quick once over. Brett asks, "Something wrong?"

"We're supposed to check 'em and I hope I have enough change this early in the day. She manages and Brett gives her a generous tip. Before leaving, he asks, "Will you be here this evening?"

Her eyes went from him to me quickly, "I'm on till twelve."

Outside, Brett looks at my disappointment and says, "If you had told me what you were going to do, I might have been more helpful."

I say, "I just wanted to see if she recognized him."

Brett grins. "That's not how you do it."

I get defensive. "Oh? You know how to, Mr. Private Detective?"

"When we come back later, I'll show you how this type of questioning is done, but this dry run has been helpful in scoping out the place and how we have to proceed."

We laze away the day and are back at the bar by nine o'clock. Our bartender is still here. We again take seats at the far end of the bar. When she asks for our order, Brett asks, "What's your name."

"Francine."

"Hi, Francine. I'm Brett and this is Taylor. Tell me, how long have you worked here?"

"A year."

"Oh, I see. No wonder you didn't recognize the man in the picture Taylor showed you earlier. He goes back five years."

Brett reaches out his hand on the bar with a fifty-dollar bill in it. She quickly spots it, takes it, and suggests, "Daisy has been here that long. Maybe you should ask her."

"Thanks a lot, Francine. Could you ask her to come over?"

"Sure."

When Daisy approaches us, she is sporting a wary look. "Hi, Daisy, I'm Brett. This is Taylor." She glances at me and nods. Brett shows her the picture with a hundred-dollar bill on top, barely concealed by his palm. She takes both and studies the photo, then looks up, "Are you cops?"

"No. But even if we were, I can assure you all we want to know is if you've ever seen this man in here before?"

She says, "Yeah. I remember him."

"Any particular reason?"

"Not really. But he came in with another guy and sat in that corner booth and worked on some paper all that night."

"By any chance, was that other guy the man who was mugged out in the alley about five years ago?"

"That's right."

"Have you seen him more recently?" Brett queries.

Daisy replies, "Sure, just last weekend, I think. But he was alone."

"Thanks very much."

We get up and leave. Outside in the car, I say, "So you've done this before?"

"No, but I read a lot of detective novels."

I say, "So now we know that my hunch was right. This is where Wes and Calvin met up five years ago."

Brett says, "How did Wes happen to find Pacific Crest?"

"Annette said he just walked in and said he was looking for a business opportunity and that's when they hooked up."

"Kind of coincidental. No?" Brett ponders aloud.

"Maybe."

"Did Annette say how far Calvin and Gabriel had advanced on the design of the new surfboard before he went missing?"

"No," I say, "I'd like to talk to the police again."

"Okay, that will be the first thing on our agenda in the morning. Right now, let's get something to eat."

I take his arm and lean in closer as we head back to the diner for burgers and fries. We are in good spirits and enjoying each other's company.

That night in the motel room, I say, "I shower at night."

He grins. "Is that something good for me to know?"

I grin back. "I take a while and I don't want to hog the bathroom."

After a long shower, I come out in a terrycloth bathrobe with my hair turbaned in a towel. We look at each other and grin. I ask, "Haven't I seen this in a movie?"

He chuckles and although he had a devilish look in his eye, I don't have anything to worry about with Brett.

In the morning, I say, "Of course you know you snore."

He replies, "So I've been told. Do you know that you whimper in your sleep?"

"No, I've never been told."

After breakfast at the same diner, we seek out the detective who handled Calvin's case in Spencer.

"Detective, I wonder if I can give a few more details on the mugging of Calvin James five years ago."

"There's not much to it. Mr. James got slugged and he wound up unconscious in the alley."

"Yes, but were there any suspects?"

"In a barroom fight? It's like cockroaches scattering when the lights go on. Nobody around to be identified. Nobody knew anybody's names. No one came forward afterward."

His wife said he always had a duffel bag with him. Was that recovered?"

He reviews the case file and after a few minutes, "No mention of it."

"Ok. Thanks. Have a nice day."

On the ride home, we review what we know. I say, "So it's pretty obvious that Wes played some part in this story. Whether or not he had anything to do with Calvin's actual attack remains to be proven."

Brett continues, "True. That's the worst-case scenario. Best case just makes him a bit sleazy. He knows poor Annette is looking for her husband and he says nothing but somehow comes up with a unique new design for a surfboard . . ."

"From which he benefits greatly in the following years," I add. "He must have known Calvin's condition to look for his business and secure a partnership in it. He had to trust Calvin wasn't about to recover soon."

"Well, you remember the medical report that was included with the police report. It said this type of amnesia didn't have a particularly good record of recovery for patients; more times than not, they don't even wake up."

I say, "Yes, I remember that. Wes must have been counting on it."

"Wes' whereabouts should be the first thing to check on back in Chelsea," Brett suggests.

Brett grows quiet as we approach Chelsea. I don't want to intrude on his thoughts, but I am curious as to what it is because it isn't like him to withdraw. "Penny for your thoughts," I say.

He stirs from his reverie. "Oh, well, I won't beat around the bush. Do you have any idea where you stand with Jake? Or what you're going to do about your marriage?"

I chew my lower lip. "He's eager to continue couples counseling and I keep telling him it's over."

"Are you going to do it? File for divorce?"

"I am."

"Well, I'd like to make a proposal because I don't want to have any influence on your timing, but I think I'm falling in love with you."

"Is that what the mischievous looks were about in the motel last night?" I ask to lighten the situation.

"No."

I am surprised.

He says, "That was pure lust and I'm old enough and wise enough to know the difference."

I smile at his wisdom.

"So, what I'm going to propose is, as difficult as it is for me, we don't see each other again until you have settled things with Jake. Either way."

I find his pronouncement shocking. But I can understand where he's coming from. He is saying, in effect, he doesn't want to fall head over heels only to have me to go back to Jake. He is a wise and prudent man. I ask myself if I prefer this type or the devil-may-care man he occasionally projected. Both. In balance.

For this reason, when Jake calls next asking to continue counseling, I tell him that I'm filing for a divorce because no amount of therapy will change my mind or my trust in him. I will tell Jake that I'll be sharing as much in our upcoming and final appointment with Roz. It's over.

Looking Ahead

I invite Jake to my next session with Roz but it's not going to be to chat about what he probably thinks. I'm done with waiting to move forward with a new future, and I'm intent on using this hour to help him understand the finality and what he needs to do too.

Knowing how a therapist conducts her or his work, I hijack the next session with Roz and tell her I want to speed up the usual exploration of feelings, pass on recounting our married lives together, and, as quickly as possible, reach some conclusion.

Roz balks, "That's not a good procedure, Taylor, and you know it. I can't go rushing either you or Jake into any conclusions. There could only be one reason you feel that way."

I have no choice but to agree with her and tell her I'm prepared for the long haul. "I know that I'll never trust Jake again and no amount of time in your office will change that or my mind."

I have my answers and I decided it wasn't necessary to play the good wife. My next stop will be with an attorney to file divorce papers. The remainder of the session was spent on Jake and talking him through his next steps to move on. At the top of the hour, we leave without exchange of words.

On my drive back to town, I call Brett and tell him I want to see him. He wants to ask questions, but I ignore his attempts and insist he meet me for lunch.

Within the hour, we are at The Perk. After sitting, he says, "Am I seeing the bossy side of you?"

"No," I say, "you're seeing the decisive side of me. Once I make up my mind, I pretty much go in all the way."

His eyes linger in mine. "I'm almost afraid . . . no, I am afraid to hear what you're going to tell me."

"You know by now that there's nothing mysterious about me. I'm an open book and what I've decided is that I will never again be able to trust Jake. But I can't live without hope of love. I need love in my life, and I know I love you, too," I confess.

He takes my hand. "All I know is the way I feel now. And that is that. If you were mine, I could never, ever let you go or take a chance on losing you."

I let my eyes lock with his. "Yes, that's what I want too."

I am feeling more like myself again, focused, energized, and ready to jump one hundred percent back into my practice. I need to follow up with Abigail before she heads north for college. I wonder how she is coping. Perhaps, she has been distracted with moving preparations enough that healing has progressed to the point where she can let go of the speculations around her mother's suicide. At least for now.

I hope that Johnston is seeking help, too. He was so emotional after sharing his secret of an affair and the child born out of it and I wonder when he will share this information with his daughter.

I check my messages on the drive to my office. One message is from Caryn. She left word that she and Darrick have separated and are working out the details of a divorce. She also thanked me for my help in pointing out that she would be fine on her own; she had her children and family nearby, and she had a job that she loved. A good support system was in place to lift her up when needed.

What was left hanging unresolved was the situation at Pacific Crest. Gabriel shared the happiness of Calvin's return has brought him. He is sleeping better, exercising more, and drinking less. He said that he was even in a committed relationship with a girl that had stuck by him through his dark and confused years. He mentions in passing that Wes had called him and was taking an official leave. He also said that he was done with the drama. "Wes was a secretive and odd fella anyway. I just want to make surfboards and commune with the ocean. To hell with all the rest."

By now, I've reached my office and disconnect from my cell phone. I am feeling re-invigorated and totally at peace with my decision to divorce Jake. I'm thinking of my future as I unlock the door to my space, the sanctuary for my clients to unburden themselves of their deepest thoughts and secrets. I step over the threshold and onto an envelope that had been slipped under the door.

I gently tear open the plain, white envelope and find a picture of Annette and me standing outside of her boutique downstairs along with a white business card with the imprint of Dr. Walter Slezak, Pediatrician neatly crossed out and below it in red ink is a hand drawn smiley face.

Panicked, I spin on my heels so fast that I lose my balance and fall into the door frame. I look right, left, but the hallway is empty. I am alone.

About the Author

Carla Tucker Minks was born in Montana and raised in Southern California. She has a BA in Creative Writing/English with a specialty in Fiction Writing from Southern New Hampshire University. *Twice Betrayed* was her first fiction novel published in 2012. This second edition will soon be followed by a sequel that continues following Taylor Calloway and her pursuits in the town of Chelsea. Carla currently lives in Arizona.

Other Works By the Author

The Adventures of Petey the Chiweenie: Learning Empathy

The Adventures of Petey the Chiweenie: Learning Sharing

The Adventures of Petey the Chiweenie: Learning Patience

The Adventures of Petey the Chiweenie: Learning Acceptance

The Truth About Dust Bunnies

The Shell

www.ingramcontent.com/pod-product-compliance
Lightning Source LLC
Chambersburg PA
CBHW030643190726
48286CB00008B/2640